Paul's Journal

Paul's Journal

KEITH DIXON

LIBERTY HILL PUBLISHING

Liberty Hill Publishing
555 Winderley Pl, Suite 225
Maitland, FL 32751
407.339.4217
www.libertyhillpublishing.com

Scripture quotations in this book were written to be true to the Bible. The language throughout, including these passages, is my own.

Paperback ISBN-13: 979-8-86850-097-8
eBook ISBN-13: 979-8-86850-098-5

Table of Contents

INTRODUCTION:

What to Expect

Paul was real and not always likeable, but he was wrestling uphill for Christ in a time of wild contention and conflict. That first century in which Paul struggled was the climax of hundreds of years of change for the Jewish world. Likeable or not, he was the one for the job.

Paul's Journal chronologically merges the Paul of Acts, his letters, and the world that Paul lived in. Additionally, Jewish history leading up to the first century played a major role in how the Jewish people of Paul's time saw their place in the world. The journal touches on some of what would have been history for Paul but includes most of it in an appendix instead of interrupting the narrative.

I wrote *Paul's Journal* to create the feeling that Paul was the author, as if it had been recently discovered. Where I thought it would help, I've acted like an editor of this recent discovery by adding headings and inserting relevant comments that Paul couldn't have known. These comments are italicized and between a set of parentheses. I also felt free to use light anachronisms where I thought it would help and not mislead readers.

The journal splits into two parts. The first four chapters follow Paul's story from the stoning of Stephen through his first Roman imprisonment, where the book of Acts leaves off. Here, I've created a biblically reliable storyline. Where incorporating Paul's letters into the Acts narrative proves difficult, I used the simplest likely solution. My focus when adding conversation and narrative color in this section was to bolster and support the biblical story, not to create new events.

The fifth and final chapter of the journal, however, is primarily based on extra-biblical material. The Bible provides only tidbits and hints about this period of Paul's life, and most of the information we have comes from later tradition. Here, I was much freer to invent stories to best reflect Paul's personality and feelings. The switch to a more relaxed approach comes very late in the journal, and I'll make sure you don't miss it.

I want to note that Paul and all the other apostles were Jewish. Their conflicts with members of the Jewish community were in this context and had the purpose of bringing them to Christ. Anti-Semitism is completely incompatible with an informed understanding of Christianity.

Finally, to the Catholic reader: I sincerely hope that you enjoy this book. I'm afraid some Catholic-Protestant issues aren't easily smoothed out. The red-flag issues for a Catholic reader in *Paul's Journal* are biblically accurate, but interpreted differently by the Catholic Church. For example, I used "James the brother of the Lord" repeatedly to distinguish him from the other James. This wording comes directly from the Bible in Galatians 1:19, but the Catholic Church interprets "brother" more broadly so that James is not the biological son of Mary. Also, I did take a little poke at papal infallibility based on the Peter-Paul conflict from Galatians 2:11-14, but, I promise, it was a good-natured poke. I hope that you too will find this book edifying.

When you finish reading this, if you have a better understanding of Paul as a real person, I'll have done my job. But for deeper Truth, I'll have to refer you to the Bible.

CHAPTER 1:

Becoming Paul

Blocking the Way

Somewhere between our initial explosion of anger and dragging Stephen to his execution site, my conceit overtook my animal desire for violence, and I began to see myself as somewhat above the fray. I slid into the role of a director or judge, above the events unfolding in front of me.

There was no reason to distinguish myself from the rest of the mob. I was just being arrogant. My haughty reserve must have shown, though, because once we were at the execution site, some men laid their coats at my feet for safekeeping from would-be thieves. Something in my demeanor told them I wasn't going to be casting the execution stones.

The rocks hit their mark, one after another. But the sounds, just mild thuds, really didn't do justice to the deed or the atmosphere in general. The rocks fell violently upon Stephen and then softly to the ground at his feet.

I had expected one solid shot to take him down – BANG, and he's out! Instead, the steady barrage weakened him slowly until he fell to his knees, crumpled to the ground, and died.

Self-righteousness is a funny sin because it hides in itself. You can make excuses for other sins or claim, "It isn't what it looks like," but self-righteousness is different; it's claiming, "It is *only* what it looks like. I act *only* out of piety." *I must have my way for the sake of God or the sake of some other good.* The self-righteous fuel their egos on a sense of acting for a greater good or purpose. It feeds the sense of moral superiority that they seek. But this moral superiority is the perfect hiding place for their true driving force, their self-righteousness. The more deeply one falls into the sin, the more hidden in itself the sin becomes.

My self-righteousness spiraled out of control at Stephen's stoning. It set my demeaner as I stood haughtily watching others throw stones, my chin tilted slightly up. I felt as if I had ordered the stoning and had command of the entire scene. As each rock-thump weakened Stephen's physical existence, it solidified this self-righteous arrogance as my self-image. I can't tell you how silly I feel looking back. After all, I was only keeping coats safe from thieves.

At Stephen's stoning, though, I became single-minded in my self-righteous sense of power: I would stamp out this Son of God blasphemy.

Stephen's Background

Perhaps I should give you a little background for Stephen's story.

Stephen belonged to the Way. He was one of the seven disciples chosen to ration food among the widows under the church's care.

Before His death, Jesus had directly appointed twelve apostles to be teachers and leaders of His Church. When Judas Iscariot committed suicide after betraying Jesus, the eleven still-living apostles appointed Matthias as their new twelfth. There had been twelve tribes of Israel, and there were again twelve living apostles of Jesus.

The number of their disciples (students or followers), however, was growing rapidly. Even some Jewish priests were accepting the gospel of Jesus. More and more Jews living in Jerusalem came to believe in the Gospel of Jesus Christ, but so too did many Jews from the dispersed, outside communities who had moved to or were visiting Jerusalem.

It's true that these people following the apostles were primarily Jews, but their different backgrounds presented challenges. Most significantly, language barriers became more of a problem. Jews from Jerusalem spoke primarily Aramaic, and the Jews from the dispersed communities spoke mainly Greek.

I only heard about this secondhand and much later, but my understanding is that when the church distributed food to its neediest members, mostly widows, some of the Greek-speaking widows were overlooked. This was apparently due to the language barrier and the expanding number of disciples. When these women complained, the apostles realized they couldn't handle the day-to-day logistics of food distribution while continuing to preach. So they told the disciples to choose seven wise and reputable men from among them, men who were full of the Spirit. These men were commissioned as community leaders to distribute food so that the apostles could devote themselves to prayer and ministry. Stephen was one of the chosen seven.

The seven men went before the apostles, who put their hands on them and prayed. I know this seems a bit dramatic for picking people to serve food, but these men were being commissioned with leadership roles in the community. The Church doesn't have any great leaders, only great servants. And so the Greek-speaking widows' complaint about food service first brought the servant Stephen forth from the crowd of disciples.

As it turns out, there was a lot more to Stephen than waiting tables. Aside from the twelve apostles, Stephen was the first disciple to perform miracles in Jesus's name. In fact, of the seven commissioned by the apostles, Stephen and a man named Phillip were the only two I know of who preached the gospel. They both preached the gospel to the Greek-speaking Jews, trying to bring them into the community of believers. Phillip even went outside of the Jewish community and baptized a high-ranking Ethiopian.

Stephen was a lot of firsts for the Church. He was one of the first seven non-apostles to be commissioned to serve the Church. He was the first non-apostle to perform miracles. He was the first murdered for faith in Jesus. What's often overlooked is that he was the first fiercely aggressive preacher without concern for social setting. Authorities breathing down your neck? Who cares? You might embarrass people? Who cares? Members of the crowd calling for your head on a pole? Who cares? Blast your message as far and wide as possible—and blast it straight through any obstacle.

This isn't at all to say that the apostles were timid and unwilling to face danger or accept the discomfort of embarrassment. But they had come up differently. They had all sat and watched and learned from Jesus and strove to emulate His gentle-but-firm approach. Like Jesus, they preached to all who came to hear them.

Stephen, like the apostles, addressed all challenges and questions directly and earnestly, with the aim of bringing the misinformed into the Way. Where they differed was in how they treated a mean-spirited accuser who was clearly not interested in knowing the Truth. Peter or the other apostles would address him softly, almost comfortingly, as if his accusation were a legitimate inquiry, "How can I be a blasphemer when Scripture tells us He will come?" Of course, the apostles knew that these accusers wouldn't hear a word; they spoke primarily for the benefit of the crowd. But their soft handling of these volatile situations kept things from exploding.

Stephen, on the other hand, would use the heckler as a springboard to do a cannonball into the crowd. To him, these situations represented an opportunity to chastise those observers on the fence and hopefully tip them into the Way by grouping them with the accuser and blasting them all for rejecting the Truth that they could see. "You Jews! You stubborn Jews!" he would yell with complete indifference to whomever the actual accuser had been.

Stephen simply couldn't be ignored. He was louder, more aggressive, more oratorical, and more condemning of those who refused to listen. Most dangerous of all, though, was that Stephen used his aggressive style to emphasize that Jesus was the Son of God. This was the ingredient that really set us devout Jews off, and Stephen just couldn't lay off it or redirect the conversation when confronted by hostile authority.

Stephen's accusers often held positions in the Jewish religious hierarchy. When their borderline-threat accusations were so unceremoniously thrust aside, the challenge to their authority left them smarting; their emotions flushed up in their faces. And because of Stephen's delivery, anyone who didn't come off the fence on the side of the Way fell off to the smarting side, and they joined the accusers in anger.

Because we Jews who didn't believe in the Way thought of it as foolish, we were initially able to suppress our anger and dispute Stephen openly, expecting to shut him down with logic. But Stephen's wisdom and the Spirit who spoke through him were too much for us to contend with. Having failed at open discourse but unwilling to let this small sect of wayward Jews continue to grow, we secretly instigated men to claim that Stephen had spoken blasphemously against God and Moses. This had the desired effect.

We Jewish nonbelievers, including the elders and scribes, were outraged by Stephen's "Son of God" claims and, more importantly, his refusal to keep these claims quietly behind closed doors (or at least deferentially hush up when confronted). We were done listening to his heretical nonsense that we couldn't quite shut down with sound logic, so we seized him to take him before the council to be tried and put to death for blasphemy. We probably wouldn't have worried about the Way if its following wasn't growing, but claiming that God had a child with some woman from Nazareth was blasphemy, plain and simple. To us, it reeked of the stories of Greek gods and mortal women.

We already knew that Stephen was guilty, so we set up articulate, if not entirely honest, witnesses to testify against him. In their testimonies, they tried to play on contemporary fears about safety from the outside world instead of what Stephen actually preached. They informed the council how Stephen went on and on, preaching against the holy Temple and the Law, and that Jesus of Nazareth was going to destroy the Temple and change the customs that we had received from Moses. Never mind that Jesus was dead, so He couldn't do these things; the blasphemy was in the claim itself. So we pressed our charges against Stephen to the council.

Until the high priest asked Stephen if the charges were accurate, we had avoided looking at the accused. His face was like the face of an angel; it was as if he had been wrapped in a purity, innocence, and grace that filled us with uneasy guilt. We all listened quietly when Stephen began his defense, if you could call it a defense.

Stephen's Defense and Death

Stephen started his defense before the council with Israelite history. "The God of Glory appeared to Abraham!" He went through Abraham, Isaac, Jacob, Joseph, Egypt, Moses, David, the Tabernacle, the Temple... To be honest, it got a bit long-winded to those of us eager for justice.

"Moses told us that God would raise up another prophet like him from among the Jewish people," Stephen reminded us. He spent a lot of time dwelling on Moses and our fathers' transgressions in the wilderness, mainly so that he could then point to Jesus as Moses and us, his Jewish accusers, as stiff-necked transgressors.

Stephen pointed directly to us, calling, "You stiff-necked people!" He compared us, his persecutors, to the ancient Jews who frequently turned from God. He had subtly but swiftly switched gears from a long-winded story to the intensely emotional and personal. He went further, declaring, "You Jews are uncircumcised in heart and ears, and resist the Holy Spirit!"

We didn't pay much attention to the "Holy Spirit" part of his statement, but the "uncircumcised" part really struck us. We knew these Nazarenes to pile up metaphors when discussing the Scriptures. But we really were supposed to be circumcised in mind as well as in body; Scripture spells this metaphor out for us in Deuteronomy: "Circumcise your heart's foreskin and stop being stiff-necked."

Stephen was arguing straight from Scripture, which we regarded as a great insult. Our self-righteousness refused to let us consider that we might be in the wrong. Thus, when accused with such a possibility, all we could do was use the charge to fuel our outrage.

We had had just about all that we could take. According to Stephen, we'd killed the Righteous One, the second Moses, just like our fathers had killed the prophets who'd announced His coming. We were untrue to our religion and only outwardly circumcised. In other words, we only went through the motions of following God without truly having our hearts in it. All these insults pushed our anger almost to the breaking point. But still, we sat seething in rage, listening and gnashing our teeth at Stephen.

With our anger at its utmost extremity, Stephen broke from his story, broke from his accusations, and shouted, "Behold! The heavens have opened, and I see the Son of Man standing at God's right hand!"

I understand why I was so furious at this shocking blasphemy, this claim that the dead Jesus was now playing God's right-hand man. What I don't understand is why this statement drove me to look down instead of up. I looked right down to the calves of the man in front of me. I even threw my hands over my ears and cocked my head in a cringe as if someone had pierced it with a sharp noise. But I refused to look where Stephen was pointing. At the time, I missed the irony that the statement about the "Son of Man" set us off when up to that point it had been the "Son of God" claim that that ignited us.

It hadn't been a conscious decision, merely a reflexive action. And this frozen, defensive posture only held me for a couple of seconds before I was, with just about everyone else there, wildly groping to get ahold of Stephen. It was about time for him to experience a real laying-on of hands! The grotesquely comical image of this Jesus, disgraced with the death of crucifixion, hanging out in heaven as God's right-hand man was really too much.

I didn't make it to Stephen, but others certainly did. To say they handled Stephen roughly would be an understatement, but they didn't attack his person with direct blows just yet. A sense of urgency drove them to drive him from the city to his punishment, his stoning. There was no waiting for an official verdict about which there could be no doubt—court was adjourned.

Once we were outside the city, a few men quickly removed their coats, tossing them at my feet so that they could better throw stones. I was content with my false sense of superiority, as if my haughty expression alone put me in a supervisory role.

As the stones hit their mark, Stephen cried out, "Lord, receive my spirit!" This delighted the wickedness inside us as if he had mocked himself for our amusement. Then he fell to his knees under the heavy barrage, but before he died, he made one last cry: "Lord, don't hold this sin against them!" These words did not amuse our wickedness but enraged it by rejecting our righteousness. Stephen collapsed dead within seconds of his prayer, but in those seconds, and even for a few seconds following, the number and speed of the rocks spiked significantly from what we took as Stephen's last insult. We could have dropped a rhino.

Stephen became the first martyr for believing in Christ. His dying prayer not only robbed us of our victory, but it also fueled our anger by highlighting the nature of the blasphemy: he had cried out a prayer to God—*our* God, not some Greek or Roman god or other new-wave stuff. These Nazarenes were claiming our God. They weren't writing a new story but stealing ours and adding heretical chapters! They were taking our most sacred beliefs, warping them in a new direction, and trying to pull us all down that Way.

Instead of feeling resolution from the execution, we were left unsatisfied and craving. Exactly what we were craving, I'm not sure. But having accomplished our purpose, we felt even emptier and hungrier. I, for one, turned myself over to a new cause: stop the gospel of Jesus Christ from spreading at all costs.

Jerusalem Persecution

It is interesting how the Holy Spirit used me at this time, even as I tried to oppose Him. Jesus had told the apostles that when they became filled with the Holy Spirit, they were to preach the Word in Jerusalem. From there, they were to spread the gospel to the ends of the earth. But as they preached in Jerusalem, how could they know when to start moving out from the city? Well, I helped beat the signal into them as we attacked the faithful so ferociously that they fled the city in droves.

I started my new anti-Christian mission by kicking in the doors of Christian homes and dragging the inhabitants off to jail—men and women alike. I was the central figure directing this persecution and fanning its fire, and I applied myself to the task wholeheartedly. I was called Saul back then, and the name filled Nazarenes with terror, which filled me with perverse delight.

This was an all-out onslaught. Stephen's trial and conviction had condemned *all* believers. He had made it clear that Christian beliefs at their core were blasphemous. It was our duty to root out these heretics and drag them in to be tried for their crimes against God. I wallowed in self-righteousness, frequently thinking of myself as a new Phineas, Eleazar's son from Scripture.

The Phineas story goes like this: The ancient Israelites were being condemned and punished by God for their transgressions. They had allowed themselves to be so seduced by foreign women that they had gone as far as bowing down to these women's gods. A prophet had just finished explaining this to a group of tribal leaders when a young Israelite, with very poor timing, walked by with a Midianite woman on their way to his tent. (I've always pictured this oblivious Israelite saying something like, "Hey, guys!" as he walked by.) Anyway, Phineas was enraged by the casual and open sin, and rightfully so. After all, it was for this behavior that God was punishing the entire community with plague. Phineas took his spear and stormed into the young man's tent. He found the two already coupled, so he drove his spear through one's back and into the other's stomach, pinning them both to the ground.

We identified with Phineas; these Christians treated our religion and our God too casually, and it was our duty to run them through. Thus, there was no direct commission or authority from public leaders to jail the heretics, but we all felt we were acting under the *ultimate* authority; we fancied ourselves an unorganized army of Phinei, acting on righteous anger.

The intensity of our onslaught drove most of the blasphemers who could escape to abandon Jerusalem and scatter about the surrounding regions. The gospel of Christ escaped with them.

Authority to Damascus

In my door-kicking campaign, I did come across some empty houses. In one such house, I found evidence that the inhabitants had fled to Damascus. Of course, Christians had been fleeing in all directions, but I latched on to a vague idea that Damascus was becoming the new Christian hotbed. Here I had clear evidence of where they had fled. It made me crazy to think that they had escaped, and I fixated on getting them back. I was so anger driven at the time, that Damascus became my obsession.

Still breathing murder against the Christians, I went to the high priest. I requested authority to go to Damascus and arrest any Christian men and women I could find there. I would bind them and drag them back to Jerusalem for trial.

Moving the onslaught to Damascus would require some planning. It was one thing to strike out at the blasphemers in the indignation following Stephen's trial, especially as the authorities were implicitly on board. But executing a city-to-city attack unsupported by the proper authority would be quite another. We never considered ourselves a mob of lawless thugs, and despite the authorities taking no blame for the violence, there was a quasi-official feel to the whole thing because it had sprung out of Stephen's trial. Plus, we weren't throwing the blasphemers off Vigilante Cliff but into prison; their cases from that point forward would be handled by the authorities.

I think I've made it clear enough that the community at large was erupting against that small group of Jews who were proclaiming Jesus of Nazareth. But as in any religious community, some members are more lukewarm than others. So here, too, were those less zealous about stomping out this heresy.

The political leaders in Jerusalem, who were technically also the religious leaders, were among the lukewarm. They were generally of the group of Jews known as Sadducees. (Like all stereotypes, this is somewhat unfair; there were zealous Sadducees too.) The high priest himself had been born and bred a Sadducee.

Stephen had stoked us all, even the lukewarm, politicking Sadducees, into a passionate blaze with his trial performance. But enough time had lapsed between Stephen's execution and my visit to the high priest that the lukewarm had cooled off, returning to their natural state of inactivity. So when I, a Pharisee Jew, approached the high priest, a Sadducee Jew, it wasn't at all clear whether he would sanction the Damascus persecution.

An interesting dynamic between our two groups meant I would never know what the high priest thought of the situation. On one hand, it is accurate to say that the Sadducees had political control of Jerusalem. They were from the city's leading families and held the position of the high priest. They were generally more comfortable with Roman authority and eager to keep up the appearance of "Everything's cool with the Jews." The council was a mix of Pharisees and Sadducees, but the council president was the Sadducee high priest.

On the other hand, the Jewish population saw the Pharisees as more piously devoted to our religion than the Sadducees. Even the less devout Jews trusted the Pharisees more because their religious dedication made them seem more Jewish than the Roman-friendly Sadducees. Thus, as the mass of the Jews had been whipped up into a club of indignation, the Pharisees had the greatest potential to wield it.

When I approached the Sadducee high priest, he may have envisioned an army of infuriated, blasphemy-crushing Jews behind me, making him feel that getting on board was really his only safe option. Or perhaps he truly was on board with stamping out the Jesus heresy. Either way, he gave me a letter to take to the synagogue in Damascus—Authority: Granted.

The Road to Damascus

I approached Damascus confidently, burning with righteousness in my mission. There were a couple of other men with me leading the donkeys, but it was my wide stride, my stern face, and my stony silence that set the tone for our trip. I was the empty, arrogant leader, the physical embodiment of the rage of the Jews; anger and adrenaline pumped through my heart as we neared Damascus. And then—BAM!

A tremendous light blasted out of Heaven, shining all around us. I fell, and as I lay on the ground, a voice filled my ears: "Saul! Saul!"

Terror and panic! I was somehow marked! Hearing my name, I knew I was totally and inescapably exposed; I wanted to scramble for cover but knew hiding was impossible. This wasn't a natural phenomenon or even general calamity sent from God; I was the sole target.

"Why are you persecuting me?" the voice asked clearly.

With this question to ponder, I was able to pull it together a bit. Even so, the best I could think to do was cry out a return question: "Who are you, Lord?" Addressing the voice as "Lord" might have betrayed that, in my heart, I knew very well who it was.

The voice answered plainly, "I am Jesus, whom you persecute." My insides slowly collapsed as the weight of understanding became too much for my soul to bear. I had supported myself with columns of self-righteousness, which now gave way. But before I was completely overcome with fear, the Lord told me to get up and go to the house of a man named Judas on Straight Street in Damascus, where I would receive further instructions.

That was it. The punch had come in, had landed, and was over. It ended so abruptly that, when I realized it, I found myself still lying face down on the road, closing my eyes tightly like a scared child.

I stood up, slowly blinking my eyes open. But I remained in darkness; I was blind. Barely controlling my panic, I whirled my head to the right and then to the left as if I could find my eyes lying upon the road. What now? Stumble blindly forward and hope to hit my target? I was still in confusion when one of my traveling companions put his hand on my shoulder and asked if I was okay.

What a relief! My confusion was so great that I'd forgotten my traveling companions. I was glad that at least I wasn't blind *and* alone in the country. This thought calmed my nerves and brought me back to my senses—well, four of my five senses, anyway. My companions and I took a few minutes to collect ourselves before we moved on.

Evidently, I had been the only one who had heard the Lord. Everyone had seen the light, but the others were as baffled by my shouting out, "Who are you, Lord?" as they were by the light itself. I was also the only one who had been deprived of sight. So much for my confident striding ahead of the two men I had led only moments earlier. I had been thoroughly humbled. My God could have justifiably smitten me. Instead, He had given me orders. God had replaced my eagerness to persecute the believers with a frantic desire to do His true will. The others led me by my hand into Damascus, to the house on Straight Street, where we settled in.

Down on Straight Street

I couldn't even guess at what the Lord would command of me. Like a child, I anticipated an unknown punishment. It didn't matter—I would do whatever He commanded. After all, even before He had appeared to me, I had thought I was acting on

His behalf. Having received direct orders, how much more boldly would I now proceed even if in a different direction? I remained blind and refused food and drink as a token of my repentance. In this condition of resignation to duty, I waited on the Lord for instruction. Then, He came to me in a vision, telling me that my sight would be restored and giving me a play-by-play of what would happen in three days when a man named Ananias would come.

After my three days of fasting and prayer, Ananias arrived at the house. I heard the knock on the door, but I couldn't make out much of the conversation between Ananias and my hosts. It didn't matter. From the vision, I knew who it was and what he was going to do next.

Ananias came over, placed his hands on me, and spoke. "Brother Saul," he said, "the Lord Jesus who met you on the road into town, has sent me so that you may see again and be filled with the Holy Spirit." At this, I felt the urge to blink. A rapid succession of blinks rubbed what felt like fish scales from my eyes. The blinking clumped them together and pushed them out. I could see! I could see the physical world, and more importantly, I could see Christ for who He was. At my blinding, I had been eager to obey God. But now, my heart was filled with Christ. To say "I understood" isn't exactly right in its nuances, but it is as close as I can come to explaining.

Jesus of Nazareth had died for my wretched sins. He had paid the debt for my transgressions. He who had been completely innocent had been sacrificed for my salvation. He had died for me, the worst of sinners and his direct persecutor. He had died, paving the path of faith, the only route to Heaven. I couldn't have saved myself with all the Pharisaical posturing in the world, even if I hadn't been acting as a Pharisee primarily for a sense of self-righteousness, superiority, and sense of community standing. It had all been pompously wasted time and effort. Jesus gave the gift of salvation to all freely.

Looking back, it seems that I should have been more confused by my healing than I had been by losing my sight. After all, a brilliant light had accompanied my blinding. But I understood God's perfect love plainly. Any confusion had fallen away with the scales of my eyes. I rose, my vision restored, and was baptized into the Lord Jesus Christ.

Ananias told us his story while I ate and drank, now in the light, slowly regaining my strength. "The Lord called to me in a vision. 'Here I am, Lord,' I answered, just like in the Scripture stories. He told me to go to Judas's house on Straight Street where I would find Saul from Tarsus. He told me about your vision, that you had seen me come in and lay my hands on you so that you would regain sight." Ananias went on, "To tell you the truth, I didn't want to do it. And I even told God so."

Ananias, of course, followed the Way. He explained to me that my name, and the suffering that I brought, were well-known in his community. They knew of everything I had done to persecute the Christians in Jerusalem. They knew I had come to Damascus with the same purpose. Because of me, they knew fear. You can hardly blame Ananias for not wanting to come and see me; there's nothing more natural than a basic sense of self-preservation. God had calmed Ananias by explaining to him that I was His chosen instrument and that He would show me the amount of suffering I would have to endure for His sake.

This comforted Ananias, and he came to me as commanded. Oddly enough, this comforted me too. That I would suffer meant little next to the fact that I would be a tool for God. To be afforded such an opportunity after having done so much wrong is a testament to God's grace.

Damascus, Desert, and the Messiah

Once those scales had fallen from my eyes, it was all I could do to take some food and engage in polite conversation with Ananias and the other disciples who were there. I was so on fire to spread the gospel that I couldn't stand it. I shot off to the synagogue as soon as I could.

I started a little clunky, preaching the gospel, but that smoothed out after only minutes the first time I addressed the people. Stephen's fire burned in me and erupted from my mouth every time I spoke. His style of preaching came so easily and naturally to me that, when I spoke, it felt like it just happened without any effort.

I stayed with the disciples in Damascus for several days, continuing to preach the entire time, leaving those Jews who refused to believe completely confounded and frustrated. When it began to look like Stephen's style was going to bring me the same result that it had brought to Stephen, and to Jerusalem for that matter, the disciples helped me pack up and hustled me out of town. I would spend the next three years wandering in the

Syrian Desert, stopping at the various villages before returning to Damascus.

(In Galatians, Paul says that he went into Arabia. In his time, the desert just to the southeast of Damascus, now the Syrian Desert, was considered part of Arabia.)

As I walked through the desert, there was so much going on in my head. Jesus of Nazareth was the Son of God. Jesus of Nazareth was the Son of Man. Jesus of Nazareth was the Messiah. God had sent the Messiah for the salvation of His chosen people. He sent His Son, His only Son, to die a horrible, humiliating death on a cross so that we may be saved. I am always mildly annoyed when fellow believers talk about how "crazy" or "unbelievable but awesome at the same time" their faith is; it really is all logical, but it's also a lot to take in.

But why was it such a shock to *me*? After all, it's not like I'd just learned about Jesus of Nazareth. Upon my conversion, no one sat down with me to explain the finer points of the faith. I'd already gleaned the main ideas from the outside as a persecutor. Plus, as a Pharisee, I believed that a resurrection would happen and that the Lord would send a messiah to deliver us Jews. (The Sadducees do not believe in these things.) How could it be that my conversion opened such a world to me? I didn't simply say, "Oops! Looks like I was wrong," and switch positions. Rather, fulfillment and a fuller-than-intellectual understanding had blossomed within me despite my past.

That the Messiah had come was so clear to me now; how had those scales clung to my eyes? The more I thought on this, the more I realized just how different the Truth was from anything that nonbelievers had ever expected. We had known nothing of *this* Messiah! As Pharisees, we expected *a* messiah, but our idea of a messiah was a revolutionary political figure who would lead us to war against the Romans. We didn't expect someone to save us from *sin*, to save us from rotting in the ground. How could the Messiah possibly be the man who had advised us to "Render unto Caesar that which is Caesar's?" You have to admit, that carries quite a different ring than "*Vive la résistance!*"

Nowhere throughout history, throughout philosophy, or throughout religion had *this* Messiah ever been contemplated. Forget Rome! Jesus of Nazareth brought freedom from sin, freedom from death itself! I walked, completely awestruck by what now appeared so obvious: Jesus the Messiah had died for my sins so that I might live.

Looking back, time in the desert was probably exactly what I needed for a complete reset. Since that time, I've seen innumerable Jews, particularly Pharisees, come to the Way and face years of desperate struggle and inner conflict over an addiction to ceremony and outward display. I imagine that it's hard for someone outside the Jewish community to understand how difficult it is for serious Jews to give up the idea that God grants His good grace to those who perform actions that He finds pleasing. For all your life, you've wanted to respect God, and you have worked hard to learn and follow His rules. Then, in almost an instant, you come to understand that you could never give enough to God to cover your misdeeds and mistakes, but He has given everything, including salvation through His Son for you. You can still follow the Jewish Law as a way to show respect, but it's not demanded, and you can't buy His favor with it. (Many, maybe most, Jews who come to Christ decide to continue following Jewish Law for this reason.) You'd expect the Jewish people who come to the Way to find relief in the lifting of their legal burden, but more often, it's just the opposite; we cling to the bondage we know. Anyway, being out in the desert and worlds away from Jerusalem and other Jewish centers made it much easier for me to break those ties.

On top of this, the desert provided ample time for contemplation. I passed much time in the wide-open spaces between villages, often just in awe of God's gift of salvation, often thinking of how to refine my delivery of the gospel. But I also contemplated the nuances of the gospel more than I had previously, which led to questions uncountable. "But then, how could this be?" I always trusted that my questions had answers, so I never veered into doubting Christ. I found the answers to many questions while in contemplation, the Christians in Damascus answered many more, and some had to wait until I returned to Jerusalem where the experts, the apostles and their close circle, could answer them.

This return to Jerusalem was not something I planned or even expected. The story of my conversion was known throughout Damascus. My complete turnaround made my story much more powerful for some, and they came to believe; but for others, that same turnaround marked me as a traitor, and they developed a special animosity for me.

When I returned to Damascus after about three years, I passed many days preaching, proving, and pushing the gospel. The believers in the city treated me politely but always seemed uncomfortable with me. I didn't really know why at the time. I didn't think it could have anything to do with my past because Ananias was so well respected that the authenticity of my conversion wasn't questioned.

In hindsight, it's clear that my style of preaching with Stephen's fire made them uncomfortable. Everything was rolling along nicely for them; they were preaching politely and gaining ground for the Lord. Then, BAM! Saul is in town with his fire and brimstone and uncomfortable volume, and *we don't think we can really say anything to him because he isn't really wrong, but if he would only tone it down...*

Before I'd been in Damascus very long, the disciples' fears began to find justification. The city held a plot to kill me.

My would-be murderers watched for me at the city gate day and night. I couldn't see any benefit to being slain, so I decided to escape by simply going around my hopeful assassins. I climbed into a basket, and the disciples lowered me to the ground through a window opening in the city wall. Everything went smoothly, and once I touched the ground, I was free to flee back to Jerusalem.

Paul's First Post-Conversion Visit to Jerusalem

Jerusalem had settled down since I had left. By the time I returned, the city was mostly calm. There were still random thug attacks against the Christians, but the Phineas mob had dissipated so that normal order under the Jewish authorities had been restored. They decided to target the Christian leaders and the more outspoken. From their perspective, they would nail the agitators who stoked the problems, but let their idiot followers go.

This was the situation when I returned to Jerusalem as a believer. Of the twelve apostles, only Peter was in the city with James, brother of the Lord. The apostles had not fled with the other believers during the Stephen persecution, but they had subsequently left for this or that reason. During the three years that I had been gone, Peter had also left town to preach in Samaria, and maybe other places for all I know, but had returned. The thought of meeting Peter and James excited me, but I worried that I wouldn't be received because of my past.

Even after three years and knowing that I professed to be a believer, Jesus's disciples overwhelmingly refused to meet me. Fear does not heal easily. Luckily, Barnabas, always positive and encouraging, made himself an exception. He was free and open with me. I expected that Peter and James would also be cold on the idea of meeting me. Barnabas, who like James was not technically one of the twelve apostles but was in their inner circle, smiled at my concern and took me straight to meet them. He explained to the others that I had seen the Lord and that I had boldly proclaimed the gospel of Jesus even into the Syrian Desert from Damascus. Far from shunning me, Peter took me into his home, where I stayed for fifteen days.

In Jerusalem, where I had caused so much trouble, I went about preaching the name of the Lord. I met every challenge to the gospel head on. I preached in Jerusalem more aggressively than needed. I can't deny that I wanted Peter and James to know how committed I was, but really, it was just how I preached; I was a Stephen. I spoke and debated throughout the city, explaining the Way to anyone who would listen.

But as in Damascus, my preaching put my life in danger. Not everyone liked what I had to say, and my earlier persecution of the believers instilled the oppressors with a special sense of hatred toward me as a traitor. I was certainly the most aggressive preacher that Jerusalem had seen since Stephen. I was starting to stir the city up again, and the most aggressive Jews, with whom I'd done so much damage three years ago, sought to kill me. In fairness to them, that would have been the only way to stop my mouth.

I had only been in Jerusalem for a short period of time, but once again, my Christian brothers learned of the plot and hustled me off to safety—that is, my safety as well as the safety of Jerusalem. My friends brought me to the nearby port of Caesarea, put me on a ship, and sent me off to Tarsus.

The plan was more to get out of Jerusalem than it was to go to Tarsus. Tarsus made sense because I was originally from there, and it was a safe enough distance from Jerusalem and Damascus that my would-be murderers would really have to commit in order to accomplish their goal. So I shipped out from Jerusalem to my town of birth.

Tarsus and the Heavenly Journey

For the fourteen years that I stayed in Tarsus, the Church as a whole was kind of in a sweet-spot period. It was an interesting time period and difficult to describe. On one hand, the threat of violence and persecution was not only ever-present but steadily building back from the lull after Stephen's stoning. Animosity against the Way was open and oppressive. On the other hand, major acts of violence like murders were no more common than they were in the Jewish community at large, and imprisonments were not something we greatly feared. In fact, in some cities, the Jews were attacked much harder than the believers. To my knowledge, after Stephen's stoning, there were no major anti-Christian riots, but the Gentiles in Alexandria exploded in riot against the Jews. *("Gentile" refers to all non-Jewish people, much like how "barbarian" was originally a Greek term that referred to all non-Greek people.)*

I didn't have any real friends in Tarsus, nor did I have a particularly warm relationship with my parents. They had cared and provided well for me as a child, but they had their things to get on with, and I had mine. Once they had sent me for instruction under the respected Pharisee teacher Gamaliel in Jerusalem, I was pretty much on my own. I've always counted myself blessed for my education, but my parents hadn't supplied me with a lot of extra cash. For that, I helped the tentmakers in Jerusalem. I did, however, get my Roman citizenship though my father, which would turn out to be quite a benefit.

Anyway, my parents and I had very little communication after I had left Tarsus. Returning, I saw them a couple of times, and it was nice to see each other in good health, but they had no interest in the Way, and our conversations felt somewhat forced. My sister lived in Jerusalem with her husband and adolescent kids, but I wasn't particularly close to her either.

I didn't have strong roots in Tarsus and never really settled in. The city was more of a home base than a home, and during this fourteen-year period I probably spent more time out of the city than in it. I traveled and spread the gospel to all the small towns and villages in Turkey surrounding Tarsus and into Syria.

Several years into my stay in Tarsus, just when comfort had begun to settle in, I was violently snatched up, never again to have a sense of earthly security. But I would ever after be instilled with heavenly joy, peace, and the ability to love. I had been snatched up into heaven.

(I don't bring this up as a braggart would, but the event's importance to my direction and efforts for the Church means I can hardly pass up writing about it here.)

When I was pulled up, I don't know if my earthly body came with me or if it was left behind. I wasn't thinking of my body at the time, but I certainly didn't notice any of the weariness the body usually carries. Because of this, some have asked me, "Are you sure it wasn't just a vision?" Yes. I was truly in Heaven. This was much more comprehensive than any vision and filled me as no vision could.

My head holds much that I'm not permitted to speak of. I haven't the ability to put much of it into words anyway. Perhaps one day the Lord will convey more to the world by showing someone more poetic than I that which He has shown me. But for now, I'm afraid you'll have to content yourself with this short version.

Being shown such may have rendered me vulnerable to conceit upon return, but I had been called with a purpose. I stood before Jesus, and He personally called me to preach as His apostle, not in the general sense of the word but meaning that I was now among *the* twelve apostles as lucky number thirteen. At His words, I suffered an intense pain in my side, which slowly subsided but never left. (The sensation was stark and real, but oddly enough, I can't say that it proves I was in body.)

I know thirteen is a clunky number, and many people challenge me on the fact that Jesus called me as the thirteenth apostle. Let me explain how this is actually kind of cool.

When Ananias had come to wash the scales from my eyes all the way back in Damascus, the Lord had told him I was to go among the Gentiles, making me officially the first to receive specific word about going to the Gentiles.

At the time, I had hardly noticed the need because so many Gentiles, though not allowed in the Temple proper, are ever-present at the Temple and synagogues. These Gentiles have taken a monotheist theology and loosely follow the Jewish religion but are usually uncircumcised and don't bother with food restrictions or other legalistic rules.

That these Gentiles would hear the message preached to the Jews was not at all shocking. Plus, believers have always been free to tell the Gentiles about the gospel—it was no secret, and what difference is there between telling and preaching? But as time went on, and it became increasingly clear that I was to preach the gospel directly to the Gentile nations, independent of the Jews, the relevance of a thirteenth apostle became evident: the twelve apostles matched the twelve tribes of Israel, and the thirteenth apostle was added on to represent the Gentiles; Jesus is open to the twelve tribes of Israel AND to the Gentiles.

The word "apostle" has been used differently over time. Originally, it referred specifically to the twelve who were hand-picked by Jesus. When Judas died, it came to basically mean those, now including Matthias, who filled the twelve positions established by Jesus. Then Jesus appointed me the thirteenth apostle, and not long after that, Barnabas and the Lord's brother James came to be called apostles in a broader sense because they were virtually indistinguishable in office and action from us. However, some people use the term too loosely to refer to any teacher or preacher of Jesus's gospel. When you hear "apostle," you need context to know what the speaker means.

Here in Tarsus, I saw my life laid out for me mainly through my experience of having been taken to Heaven, but day-to-day life filled in the gaps. I was commissioned by the Lord to spread the gospel, develop communities of believers, and strengthen them in the faith.

Establishing communities would come with a burden, a sense of responsibility for these communities. The Adversary *(the Devil)* would stir up problems within them, endeavoring to destroy my work for the Lord *through* my work for the Lord. Time and again, the communities of believers I established would falter in strife, animosity, and glory-seeking, among other things.

(That through these sins, the churches would further the Adversary's work pierces me beyond a metaphorical, emotional piercing; I suffer an intense shot of physical pain in my side with every epidemic outbreak of sin in any of the local churches I've established. This physical jolt, every time it comes, knocks me down a peg by reminding me that I'm not some great orator meant for talking alone, divorced from the actions of these communities; I am responsible for these churches. And every time one fails, it reflects failure on my part to some extent. Those churches would be my joy, but they would also be the thorn in my side.)

The responsibility of this commission left me flabbergasted, and I pleaded with the Lord to find someone else to take it. I was honored, of course, but in no way up to the task. To my plea, the Lord simply replied that His grace was enough and that His power was perfected in weakness. How ridiculous would *any* argument against the sufficiency of His grace be? On the other side of the coin, what human *could* be up to the task without His grace? I, Paul, now one of the thirteen apostles of the Lord, accepted my commission to establish the Church of the Lord, even among the Gentiles.

In the Syrian Desert and Damascus, I had acted as a lone prophet of old, just wandering about, declaring the Word of the Lord. I had proclaimed the gospel freely, but I hadn't made any real effort to establish a community of mutual support among believers. In fact, the thought hadn't even crossed my mind. My faith was strong, and my desire was strong, but I was an infant of a believer. I ran around, cranking out the Word to as many people as possible. But I didn't make any serious effort to get to know these people or help establish community among them.

In Jerusalem, Peter and James had shown me perfect Christian kindness. Even my being universally shunned by all of the other disciples there did not come from animosity but from discomfort regarding my past. Spending that time with Peter, I got a picture of a kind and gentle community. When they did argue or become angry, they were so eager to apologize that they would almost start fighting over who got to be at fault. It was the attention I received from Peter and James, but especially from Peter, that opened my eyes to the importance of developing a community into a system of mutual support; people need attention. Believers, especially community leaders, work together not just to spread the Word as wide and as fast as possible but also to keep the individuals of the flock safely in the Way.

I brought this image of a healthy, functioning Christian community to Tarsus with me and absorbed it as a model, which I tried to emulate. I made a conscious effort to seize opportunities to help and encourage others during my time in Tarsus. These traits seemed to come so easily to Peter, but I really had to work on them. Peter made it seem like kindness and living in community were part of human nature, but it sure didn't come naturally to me. I had to work to learn to love and give freely, and Tarsus was my training ground.

Peter's Corresponding Vision

Quite some time after I left Jerusalem for Tarsus, Peter was also called out of the city. He performed many healings, signs, and wonders along his way. In Joppa, he even revived a woman from death, which I have to admit shocked me when I first heard of it.

One day while Peter was in Joppa, he went up on a rooftop around noon to pray. While he was up there, he had a vision or fell into a trance, but he was not taken up to Heaven like I was. In his vision, something like a great sheet was let down by its four corners, which contained mammals, reptiles, and birds. The books of Moses forbid the Jewish people to eat certain kinds of animals. We call these animals "unclean," so, of course, those we can eat we call "clean." Peter's sheet from heaven contained all types of animals, both clean and unclean. When the sheet landed, a voice told him to get up, kill something, and eat. Peter stated that he had never eaten anything common or unclean in his life, but the voice replied firmly, "What God made clean, do not call unclean."

The vision perplexed Peter, a devout Jew and follower of Jesus. As he contemplated it, two men arrived asking for him. The men had been sent by a Roman centurion named Cornelius, an upright and God-fearing man who was one of the Gentile monotheists following Israel's God. An angel had told Cornelius to send the men to Joppa to get Peter and bring him back to Cornelius's home in Caesarea.

In Caesarea, Cornelius had called together friends and family to hear whatever Peter had to say because an angel had foretold his coming. When Peter arrived, Cornelius dropped to the ground to worship him. But Peter lifted him back to his feet, saying, "I am a man just like you, the same under God. From what God has shown me, I can never call any person, even a Gentile, common or unclean. God doesn't show partiality, and anyone from any nation who fears Him and does right is acceptable to Him."

Peter went on to preach the gospel of the Lord to Cornelius's household, and the Holy Spirit fell upon the Gentiles in divine confirmation of God's acceptance. Some of them even began speaking in tongues. The entire household was baptized in Christ our Lord.

(It's not super important, but I should also point out that because I was called to preach to the Gentiles when I was in the house on Straight Street, I was technically called to preach to the Gentiles before Peter was, even though my being taken up to Heaven and Peter's rooftop vision happened at about the same time, and we can't really be sure which happened first. Not a big deal, but I thought you should know.)

Antioch

The believers who had scattered throughout the known world, especially after the Jerusalem persecution, preached the gospel everywhere they settled. But Peter's story about Cornelius and the Holy Spirit falling upon the Gentiles had not yet made it to these dispersed believers. Consequently, they didn't yet know to reach out to the Gentiles; they had almost uniformly focused their gospel preaching on other Jews.

The Spirit, however, chose to make a major exception in Syrian Antioch. Here, the Gentiles had also received the gospel, and a great many of them accepted it by turning to the Way.

When the Stephen persecution forced so many believers from Jerusalem, some from Cyprus and others from North Africa fled to Antioch. These more cosmopolitan believers were joyously open and free with the gospel, and the Gentiles flooded to the Way. The church in Antioch, unlike any other location at that time, was loaded with Gentile believers.

It's not exactly clear why the Holy Spirit decided to bring the Syrian Antioch Gentiles into the Way in such numbers before the Gentiles of other areas, but Syrian Antioch is the largest city within the boundaries of the Promised Land and the third largest in the known world. It could serve as headquarters for the Church if Jerusalem, as a Jewish center hot with emotions, proves too chaotic for an administrative base.

When the apostles in Jerusalem heard of all the Antioch Gentiles who had turned to the Way, they were greatly encouraged in their mission to spread the gospel. So they sent Barnabas, a Christian leader filled with the Holy Spirit, to Syrian Antioch to preach the Way.

Barnabas thus brought ever more Gentiles to the Way while I was still proclaiming the Lord in Tarsus. Then Barnabas came to Tarsus for me. I was happy to see this Church leader who had first trusted me and introduced me to the other apostles in Jerusalem. He brought me back to Antioch, where we taught together for an entire year. Here, the roots of the Church grew deep.

Antioch is also where we were first called Christians, often derogatorily by non-Christians, but the natural name for the "followers of Christ" stuck. How could a follower of Christ really complain about being called a Christian? It's probably not a coincidence that the term was first applied at this notably Gentile Christian location. It may represent the very beginning of Christianity being seen as separate from Judaism by the outside world, but it was quite some time before Christianity was universally seen as distinct.

During that year in Syrian Antioch, my relationship with Barnabas grew as fast as the number of local believers grew. Barnabas had always been a bit of a mentor to me. For all my fortitude in the face of persecution, for all the strength of my faith, even for my having been commissioned directly by our Lord and Savior Jesus Christ, my image of Barnabas as among the apostles caused me to fall into the role of a follower, or number two. The dynamic worked at the time.

James, Brother of John, Killed

While we were in Antioch, we received news from Jerusalem that James, the brother of John, had been killed.

At this time, the concept of the messiah as a rebellious political leader was every bit as popular as it is now, but the "Christian Messiah Philosophy" wasn't understood by many non-Christians. It wasn't uncommon for individuals to pop up out of nowhere claiming to be the military messiah, then gather a following and lead them out to be crushed by the Romans. Because of our belief in the Messiah of true salvation, many people confused Christians as being one of these groups. (Sometimes, at a Christian's trial for a seemingly trumped-up charge, you can see the frustration on the accuser's face when the Christian wholly admits to believing in the Messiah but then denies supporting rebellion against Rome; the charges seemed as obviously false to the Christians as obviously true to the authorities.)

Herod Agrippa I, the king and the grandson of Herod the baby-killer, may not have been as paranoid as his grandfather, but he stayed constantly on his guard against any potential threat. As a king, he was ready to shut down any would-be messiah movement, especially one growing as quickly as the Christian Church.

When Agrippa ventured to Jerusalem for the Passover, the Jews most put out by the Christian Church bombarded him with stories of brazen Christian wickedness. The two names most often on their lips were James and Peter. Somehow Peter got a temporary pass while James, the brother of John, was arrested. Since Passover would soon forbid executions, urgency made his seizure and conveyance to court a hasty matter.

A haggard jailor led James before Agrippa and stood next to him during the short trial. Because of the messiah confusion, the trial seemed to focus on simply whether James was a Christian; no other specific crime was mentioned. Of course, given this public platform, James loudly declared that Jesus Christ is Lord and Savior before giving a short sermon.

Tears streamed down the jailor's cheeks. "I confess! I confess!" he yelled. "Jesus Christ is my Lord and Savior! Jesus Christ died for my sins! He is the Messiah of true salvation!"

The room sat in astonishment, but Agrippa quickly regained himself and knew how to deal with the situation. The two new brothers wanted to lose their heads together? Two executioners would be appointed so that they could lose their heads at the same time. Just before the two Christians were taken to their deaths, those who watched saw James kiss the other man, his jailor-turned-brother, gently on the forehead.

At the close of James's trial, the Jews who had encouraged his arrest showered Agrippa with flattery, which he felt was well deserved. Feeling inflated and wanting to ride the wave from his flatterers, he ordered Peter to be arrested and brought before him.

Peter's Arrest in Jerusalem

Shortly after Passover, we received more news: Peter had been arrested. But the news came with a twist.

Peter's arrest came quickly after James's execution, but it still came too close to Passover to safely rush his trial and execution. There was no way Agrippa I was going to risk his image, not to mention the anger of the Jews, just to execute some Christian during Passover when it was ritually forbidden. While he might have been a wild playboy in Rome, here in Jerusalem, King-Politician Agrippa played the part of perfect piety. Peter could wait in prison until after Passover.

As Peter slept, locked in chains between two guards, he woke in a dream to an angel of the Lord striking him in the side. "Get up!" the angel said. "Quickly! Get dressed and get your sandals on." His chains fell from him, but that feeling of stupor did not as he coasted through the angel's directions. He followed the angel past the prison gate, which had swung open of its own accord, and into the city street. Here, the angel disappeared. Slowly, Peter's sense that he was in a dream also disappeared. There he stood, alone and looking rather silly in the middle of the street in the middle of the night.

Peter made his way to the hours of Mary, mother of Mark, stopping briefly to leave a message for James, the brother of the Lord, before going to a safer house for the night. In the morning, he fled to Caesarea.

Herod Agrippa ordered all of Peter's guards killed for taking bribes. Then he, too, went to Caesarea for reasons completely unrelated to Peter. The people of Sidon and Tyre begged Agrippa to come and settle a dispute that he had with them because he basically controlled their food supply. When Agrippa told the people that he would not starve them to death, they cheered him and proclaimed him a god. He liked this very much until he saw an angel of the Lord come to smite him with disease. Like his grandfather's, his bowels began to be eaten by worms even before his soon-to-follow death.

Paul's Second Post-Conversion Visit to Jerusalem

While we were in Syrian Antioch, prophets came from Jerusalem. One of the prophets, named Agabus, foretold great famine that would cover the entire world during Roman Emperor Claudius's reign. So the Christians in Syrian Antioch decided to preemptively send relief to the brothers and sisters in Judea and put Barnabas and me in charge of bringing those provisions back to the church in Jerusalem.

It was a simple task, but I found it very gratifying. I know it's silly and perhaps overly sentimental, but this couple of years with Barnabas may have been the only time in my adult life when I felt free to relax and follow the lead of another. I was past wanting to be seen as the leader and was comfortable with Barnabas's ability, so I didn't feel irresponsible for not taking charge. I look back particularly at this little trip with great pleasure.

After we delivered the supplies in Jerusalem, Barnabas's cousin Mark made the return trip to Syrian Antioch with us.

CHAPTER 2

Jewish–Gentile Relations and Paul's First Two Missionary Trips

First Missionary Trip (with Barnabas): Cyprus

(Commentators on the book of Acts often discuss Paul's three missionary trips, which sometimes leads to the impression that the three trips are the extent of his work. However, these three missionary trips are smack in the middle of his story. What commentators call "Paul's First Missionary Trip" starts here, after about fifteen years of evangelical work.)

While we teachers and prophets were worshiping and fasting in Syrian Antioch, the Holy Spirit told the group to set Barnabas and me to a special task. We were to be sent off together on a mission to spread the gospel and establish the Church. The others laid their hands on us and prayed. We assembled a small team, including Mark, to accompany us, and without any delay, we were off to the nearest port city. There, we boarded a ship sailing to the large island of Cyprus.

When we arrived, we disembarked at the city of Salamis, which had been named after the more famous island where the Greeks defeated Xerxes and the Persian Navy over 500 years ago *(480 BC)*. Barnabas was from Cyprus, so this island held a special place in his heart. More than a decade after this visit, Barnabas would settle here in Cyprus, only to be stoned by some inhabitants of his beloved Salamis *(about AD 61)*.

From Salamis, we worked our way through the entire island. We proclaimed the gospel of Jesus in the synagogues until the attention that we received caught the Roman proconsul Sergius Paulus's curiosity, and he summoned us.

As we were delivering the message of Christ to the proconsul Sergius, that devil Elymas sat on his other shoulder, offering him twisted counsel. This Elymas, a false prophet and magician who had wormed his way into the proconsul's circle of advisers, worked his tongue, trying to turn Sergius from the true faith.

I wasn't having any of it. Filled with the Holy Spirit, I glared at him and called him out, more for Sergius's sake than his own: "You son of the devil! You enemy of righteousness! Deceitful villain! You make the straight paths of the Lord crooked! Behold! The Lord's hand is upon you! You will suffer short-term blindness." I'm not sure where that last bit came from. The words flowed from my mouth so smoothly, without a thought.

The magician's sight was instantly taken from him; misty vision and then total darkness swallowed him—very fitting when you consider that, as a magician and false prophet, he had lived in an even deeper darkness for years. Elymas stumbled about, looking for someone to lead him by the hand, but no one rushed to help the magician who had fallen under God's punishment. Sergius stared on in amazement and believed in the gospel of the Lord.

(About the time of this great miracle, the book of Acts begins using the name "Paul" instead of "Saul." Modern scholarship, of which I am skeptical, asserts that Paul is a more common and easier name for Greek speakers, and the change was because Paul is now venturing farther out into the Greek world. In the Scriptures, however, name changes are significant, pivotal moments in individuals' lives and relation to God. For examples, Abram became Abraham when God made a covenant with him, and Jacob became Israel after wrestling with God. Traditionally, Saul became Paul when he became a Christian on the road to Damascus.)

Turkish Antioch: The First Sabbath in the Synagogue

(The landmass that we call Turkey was not a single geo-political unit called Turkey in Paul's time. It was about half a dozen smaller units, including Galatia and Lycia, to name a couple. I have Paul refer to these geopolitical units as "Turkey" to minimize confusion.)

With my companions, I set sail for Turkey. This was where Mark decided to split. He went back to Jerusalem, cutting out on the bulk of the work yet to be done on this missionary trip. Barnabas and I went to the Turkish city also called Antioch. (Turkish Antioch is much smaller than Syrian Antioch, which had developed such a strong Christian base.)

On the Sabbath, Barnabas and I went into the synagogue and sat down. After the readings from the Law and the Prophets were finished, the synagogue rulers directed us to encourage the people with any words that we had. I stood and motioned with my hands to signal that I was about to speak.

I gave a brief sermon, starting with the history of Egypt and working down to Saul and David. Over time, Moses had become a favorite starting point for these discourses—at least, we tended to focus on him because Moses was known as the intercessor for the Jews, especially when they really needed it. (Now that Jesus had died for our sins, Moses has basically been replaced by Jesus as the perfect intercessor. At least, it is a great comparison for a Jewish audience.)

Next, I moved into the meat. I introduced Jesus as having come from David's line, explaining that this Jesus was the Savior proclaimed by John the Baptist. I announced to them all that the salvation message had been fulfilled.

Then, adding a hint of warning, I boldly stated that the Jewish leaders didn't understand the prophecies in the Scriptures they read from every Sabbath. And because they didn't understand the prophecies, they fulfilled them by killing Jesus the Savior and Intercessor, the perfect Moses, by hanging Him on the cross. I explained that when Jesus was taken down and entombed, He rose from the dead three days later. I announced the good news that God had promised our fathers and even quoted the old Scriptures for their benefit. I leaned heavily on the Scriptures, using the Jews' familiarity with these writings to help them understand the Gospel more fully.

Drawing near the end of my sermon, I spelled it out for them: Through Jesus, your sins are forgiven. And by Jesus, all who believe in Him are freed, even from that which the Law of Moses could not free us.

My words seemed to have gone over quite well. As we left the synagogue, people begged us to come back and talk more about salvation through Christ on the next Sabbath. And many of the devout Jews and the converts to Judaism followed us out of the synagogue to talk with us. Things were looking good.

Turkish Antioch: The Second Sabbath in the Synagogue

The next week, nearly the whole city gathered at the synagogue. Word had gotten out. At first, we were thrilled with such an audience, such potential to bring people to the Way of Christ. Unfortunately, the massive crowd, which had obviously turned out because of our presence, made some of the Jews jealous. They spoke out against us, trying to contradict and insult us. They were quite content with their pre-gospel world and not eager for any change or challenge.

Barnabas and I had always spoken out boldly concerning the gospel. That boldness didn't fade a bit, but when it became clear that our progress in the synagogue had reached an end, we called it for what it was. Exasperated by the persistent stubbornness and aware that we couldn't push our words into closed ears, we bailed on converting these Jews. We announced that it had been necessary to speak God's Word to the Jews first but that they had thrust it aside, counting themselves unworthy of eternal life. Wrapping up, we told them flat-out that we would now turn to the Gentiles.

Upon hearing this, the Gentiles rejoiced at their inclusion in the community of the one true God. Many glorified God by accepting the gospel of the Lord; they believed and found eternal life. The Word of the Lord spread throughout the entire region. Exactly how far or fast was anyone's guess.

Unfortunately, as positive as the reaction was among the Gentiles, the reaction from the Jews seemed negative to the same degree. They incited men and women of high standing in the city against Barnabas and me. The Jews drove us out of the city with their hostility, which had not yet turned to physical violence. As to these Jews, we simply knocked the city's dust from our feet and moved on to nearby Iconium.

Iconium

As had become our habit, once we arrived in Iconium, we first went to the synagogue and spoke there. Again, we had some initial success and brought a lot of people to the Way. But again, nonbelievers stirred up hostility and used false reason to poison hearts and minds against the gospel. Their cry was always the same no matter where they raised it: "Blasphemy! Stop your ears in fear of the Lord! You haven't the capacity to decide this issue for yourself! Listen only to the respectable orthodox Jews who know the will of God!"

Here at Iconium, Barnabas and I were able to bring Jewish and Gentile nonbelievers together for a common cause.

Unfortunately, this cause was to oppose us. At first glance, their alliance would seem a bit odd when you consider that the two groups had completely incompatible religious beliefs. They were, however, willing enough to set aside these beliefs to form a monotheist–polytheist alliance against our upsetting the status quo. Both the Jews and the Gentiles revolted against the gospel, proclaiming us terrible blasphemers who could not be permitted to continue.

I daresay that the absurdity of this alliance for its purpose caused many to wonder if maybe there was something special about this new gospel after all. Either way, we stayed and spoke boldly, performing signs and wonders with our hands and healing the sick in the name of Jesus.

The chasm between the faithful and the rest of the city grew deeper and wider, and those hostile to us became increasingly aggressive. This group of Jews and Gentiles, including their rulers, initially seemed content to verbally abuse us. Soon, though, their verbal onslaught gave way to physical aggression until occasional rocks landed against our bodies. Iconium was the first place where I suffered real, life-threatening, physical abuse for my faith, though the threat of violence had been ever present.

That first rock hit my forearm, which I had raised with an instinctive cringe to block the incoming missiles. When it hit me, the image of Stephen standing boldly against an angry onslaught of rocks came into my head, and I was unafraid. (I find it interesting how Stephen's memory strengthens me instead of causing me the shame I deserve.) All the same, it was clear to me that being martyred there would have brought little good to the Kingdom. The Lord planned more work for us, so we fled. We fled without fear, but also without wasting time, to the surrounding countryside. More hopped-up on adrenaline than run down by pain, we then made our way to the city of Lystra.

Lystra

In Lystra happened one of the most ridiculous situations that I've ever been in.

There was a man who had never been able to use his feet. As he sat listening to me proclaim the gospel, concentrating on my every word, I set my attention directly on him. I could tell he had the faith to be made well. So, with my eyes still fixed on him, I boomed out, "Stand on your feet!" He shocked the crowd when he stood and walked.

At this point, things got crazy. Normally, when the Holy Spirit performs a sign or wonder through my hands, it sparks interest and excitement among the onlookers, giving me a warm audience to whom I can deliver the gospel. By then, we had performed so many wonders in so many places that it had become almost routine. The people would see the wonders, realize we weren't just blowing smoke, and turn to the gospel of Jesus the Christ. I had expected to follow the same preach-and-perform-wonder pattern here. But that's not what happened.

At first, we really had no idea what was going on in the excited chaos of the mob. I had healed a man crippled since birth, causing a great stir. But, for all the excitement, the people weren't listening to the gospel. And all the chatter was just that to us; we couldn't really understand their dialect as they rattled on excitedly.

Then the pagan priest's actions clarified the situation. When we saw him bringing an ox and garlands, we realized that they intended to sacrifice to us. They actually thought we were a pair of their petty gods! Despite everything we had said and done, they thought that I was Hermes and that Barnabas was Zeus. (Evidently, I still had a bit of the underling image going for me. God, forgive me for being a little jealous that Barnabas got Zeus.) Had we sought personal glory or wealth and not to spread the gospel of our Lord, here was a chance to seize dishonest and damning gain, if ever there was such a chance.

Barnabas and I acted in unison without having to consult one another. We tore our clothes and rushed into the crowd. *(Ripping clothes was an outward sign that the locals would understand as Paul and Barnabas seeing the people's acts as horrifically tragic and deeply emotionally wounding to them.)* We cried out, begging them not to behave so foolishly and wickedly. We asked how they could possibly think we were not mortal men just like them. We tried to redirect their attention from their vain things, their gods, to the Living God who had made Heaven and Earth. We went on and on, preaching that the nations had been permitted to walk in their own ways before but that the rains from heaven and the fruitful seasons were all from Him—the one true God. Still, we were barely able to restrain them from sacrificing the ox to us mortal men.

Disappointment settled on the crowd; they received the gospel as rain on their parade. They had been so excited to think us gods that they took the miracle we had performed and eternal salvation as letdowns. This made them easy targets for those who wanted to discredit us.

Jews had come from Turkish Antioch and Iconium to stop us from spreading the gospel of the Lord. Some of them had traveled over one hundred miles by road just to oppose the Way. They wished to wrap up some unfinished business from Iconium and so persuaded the crowd to stone us.

The rocks came much harder than they had in Iconium. This time, I really noticed the sound. Unlike the mild thumps at Stephen's stoning, these rocks seemed to come in against my body with heavy thuds, the pain amplifying the sound. Again, I thought of Stephen's death and the glory that he had given to God by praying for his attackers, by loving and trying to save them even as they were in the process of killing him.

A wave of excitement swept over me as I expected to receive the same opportunity that Stephen had, but a chance to talk never opened. After the short barrage of the loud thumps and thuds, there came a higher-toned crack against the side of my head, near my temple. I remember the shot of pain. I remember the ringing tone. I remember the fuzzy blackness overcoming my vision and the droning tone overcoming my senses. And that was it—I was out.

I came to several hours later with my head throbbing and my body sore. Having been taken for dead, I was dragged by my attackers out of the city and dumped to rot. I had no idea if Barnabas had made it out alive or how any of the others had fared. Several believers were with me when I awoke, and some of them left to collect my colleagues while I collected my wits. Then together, the living Barnabas included, we marched back through the gates and into the city.

I knew that the city was lost, or at least that there wasn't any more work for us to do there, but going back into the city seemed important. It was a way to announce that I had not been killed and that the gospel of the Lord was something they would not be able to stop. News that I had reentered the city, alive and unafraid, would spread. Those drawn to the Word but still on the fence would hear and be strengthened by the news. I wasn't about to needlessly surrender my life, but I wasn't going to run off with my tail between my legs either, especially when there was such potential good to come from news of my quiet return.

I had been stoned for boldly preaching the gospel, and I would continue to boldly preach the gospel. The people of Lystra would know that they could not dim the glory of the Way or my commitment to it. But there was no more reason to preach to crowds in Lystra. I moved on from the city that foolishly claimed me a god before foolishly claiming me a heretic.

Derbe & the Return Trip

The next day, Barnabas and I left for Derbe, another city in Turkey. We preached and brought people to the gospel there, but Derbe signaled the end of the line for this missionary trip. Barnabas and I both just knew it was time to return to Jerusalem.

However, instead of heading straight back to Syrian Antioch for easy passage over land, we decided it would be better to backtrack the way we had come. Despite the wild ride we had received from those who rejected the Way, in each of the communities we had visited, people had also accepted it. We would revisit these communities of new believers to strengthen them. These Christians belonged to the body of Christ, and neglecting them after bringing them into the Way would have been to neglect my missionary duty by leaving their new faith unshored.

So back we went to all those places that had greeted us with that uneven mixture of welcome and wanton abuse—back through Lystra, Iconium, and Turkish Antioch. Unfortunately, though, there was no convenient ship back to Crete, so we skipped that stop. Our purpose was to strengthen and encourage our friends to continue in the faith. Preaching to nonbelievers was a lesser priority this time, so we experienced little difficulty on the return trip. We appointed elders in every church with prayer and fasting and committed them to the Lord.

We made our way through the countryside and the cities, to port and sea, and finally found ourselves back in Syrian Antioch. Having finished the work that God had called us to do on my first major tour, we settled here for a good long time.

The Circumcision Rift

Some believers came from Jerusalem to spread the gospel while we were in Syrian Antioch. But they were teaching that you had to be circumcised before you could be saved. Barnabas and I debated extensively with them, but they would not see the Truth of the matter: there is no circumcision requirement for salvation. They were dead set on overturning the freedom we had in Christ, arguing that faith was useless without circumcision.

(You have to remember, to the Jews, circumcision is a fundamental requisite for God's chosen people. It is the most important outward sign of being in covenant with God. This is something that even those Jews who came to believe in the Way had a hard time giving up, especially the legalistically-minded Pharisees. It isn't that these believers were thoroughly evil, but the Adversary was certainly using them to stifle the freedom of Christ.)

The circumcision-before-salvation call was going up throughout the community of believers, causing a major disturbance. Not to require circumcision diminished the importance of the Jewish believers' most cherished tradition, but requiring circumcision invalidated Gentile believers' salvation without the knife. This issue needed to be settled definitively for the Kingdom as a whole. Barnabas and I headed for Jerusalem with the Gentile believer Titus and several other appointed people from the local church to discuss and settle the matter with the church leaders there.

On our way to Jerusalem, we told anyone we could about how the Gentiles were being converted to the gospel. This information spread great joy and, I hope, helped spread the word about the Gentiles' acceptance into the Promise. The genuine welcome we received from the believers in Jerusalem couldn't ease the tension from the situation, though. The believers who had come to the Way from the Pharisee sect of Jews were especially on their guard. (When I had been a Pharisee, I wallowed in the outward signs of religion, social standing, and the self-righteous feelings of being pious. I don't really relate to the Pharisees who become Christians and continue to find rich meaning and humbleness before God from Pharisee practices.)

To be honest, it was even difficult for me to relax, lest I let my own guard down. I had overwhelming evidence that the Gentiles were welcome as part of God's covenant people. But what if I'd misinterpreted the situation? I desperately desired James and Peter to give me their hands in fellowship on this issue, but if I was wrong in some nuance, it was time to set the record straight. The rock and the hard place that I found myself between were knowing that I was 100 percent right but also knowing I had to stay 100 percent open to the Holy Spirit for guidance. I resolved to put forth all my evidence in Jerusalem with my clear, unwavering conviction on the issue. At the same time, I would be careful to not make it a personal goal or a fight for my own desires. His will be done.

So we believers met in an open gathering in Jerusalem. The believers who had come to the Way from the Pharisees were noticeably edgy and eager to defend their position. The entirety of their social standing and their identity had been formed on their knowledge of and strict adherence to the Law. To surrender the circumcision issue would be to surrender everything they had held so dear and worked so hard for as Jews devoted to God. They wasted no time but quickly spoke up, stubbornly asserting that circumcision and keeping the Law of Moses were essential for salvation. We found ourselves in a situation with two groups of fiercely committed believers with no middle ground to meet on.

The Jerusalem Council

Because of this deadlock, Barnabas and I broke off with the other apostles and elders to consider the matter in what we hoped would be a more productive setting. This was much more orderly, as there were fewer of us and we were all mature Christians, but we still seemed stuck in a stalemate. Everyone knew the arguments thoroughly and had chosen sides.

Finally, Peter stood up and repeated the same line that had already failed to change the pro-circumcision minds; he droned on that God intended the Gentiles to also receive the gospel and believe. He calmly explained, as if the pro-circumcision party hadn't already considered it, that God had given the Holy Spirit to the Gentiles also and not to us Jews alone. Then he slammed his point down like a hammer: "Why would you test God by saddling these believers with the burden of circumcision and the Law when even our Jewish fathers couldn't handle such a burden? In the grace of the Lord Jesus Christ will these believers find salvation, not in the Law."

Of course, I had already known this and agreed with Peter. But when he put it like that, I had a moment of shocking clarity. The difficulty of religious perfection is clear enough, but the incredible fact that Jesus had perfected the Law struck me in all its rich glory like never before.

Jesus, as He Himself said, didn't overturn the Law but fulfilled it. A life of debauched anarchy didn't become an option as it would have if the Law had simply been overturned. But through His life, death, and resurrection, Jesus satisfied the requirements of the technical Law for all who followed Him, so they need not go through formulaic procedures.

Even if the Law were a means to salvation, no human would ever be saved by it because no human alone could ever follow it fully. The salvation of Christ is directly incompatible with any formal legal requirements as part of salvation.

I'm not sure if Peter's statement had impacted the others present for the same reason that it had impacted me, but it had clearly resonated with them too. The statement washed the confidence from the faces of the circumcision party.

I took this as my cue, so I tapped Barnabas on the arm. We stood up and started speaking quietly. Everyone else remained silent, and we told them about the signs and wonders God had done through us among the Gentiles. Again, we weren't announcing anything new, but Peter had started the ball rolling, and I thought it important to keep it moving in the right direction. Plus, refreshing the facts of uncircumcised conversion while minds were still reeling from Peter's statement might help them to settle down on the proper track. As soon as we were done speaking, James, brother of the Lord and head of the Jerusalem church, stood.

James had the attention of all when he stood. When the other apostles had left Jerusalem, James had stayed to fill a leadership role in the local church. We all respected James. And because he scrupulously followed the traditional Jewish Law, his credibility was very high, even within the circumcision party and those bent on enforcing the Law.

When James stood, we felt he would now settle the issue if he, too, objected to circumcision as necessary for salvation. But we also knew that we had already given our best arguments. If James found the Law fundamental to following Jesus, an irreparable schism might rip between the Jewish believers and the Gentile believers.

Before citing Scripture, James reminded us of the news Peter had given us: that God was also with the Gentiles. This was a great start, but I knew James was full of "However" when he spoke, so I was still nervous.

James ultimately concluded that we shouldn't bother the Gentile believers with the Law of Moses in general, including circumcision. He did toss a "However" out, but it wasn't objectionable to any individuals who were present. We were simply to admonish the new believers to abstain from several things: things polluted by idols, sexual immorality, strangled animals, and animal blood.

The Gentiles shouldn't eat food sacrificed to idols, participate in orgies, or otherwise wallow improperly in the flesh. You just can't intentionally benefit from the worship of other gods or live in a state of self-debasement and expect to be close to the Holy God. The Gentiles should also not eat animals killed by strangulation, which is likely to promote a lust for cruelness in people. They should also make sure to drain the blood before eating an animal because the life is in the blood, and consuming it is too close to the darker pagan rituals.

These requirements, of course, already applied to the Jewish people. Thus, in order for Gentiles to become Christians, they had to accept some Jewish rules, which may have made it easier for the circumcision party to yield. This was not a compromise, however. Although circumcision was a more hotly debated subject, these prohibitions are more fundamental to a relationship with God the Creator, not of ceremony but because violation of these rules necessarily distances you from God. These rules serve to sharply distinguish Jews (and now Christians) from the pagan world.

Our brothers who used circumcision and the Law as a barrier to salvation slowly began to nod in assent after James had finished speaking. They weren't necessarily happy to have fallen on the losing side of the issue, and their nods were certainly not vigorous, but they were nevertheless convinced that we had come to the right decision, and they did not resent it. Barnabas and I, with the support of Peter and James, had won over their minds to the Truth. There is, however, no doubt that it was primarily James's position that tipped the scales in our favor. After all, if there is one thing those of Pharisee heritage understand, it's respect for people who follow the Law as well as James does.

A letter was drawn up to inform the church in Syrian Antioch of our results. Barnabas and I then delivered it personally to Syrian Antioch, accompanied by Titus and a few other believers so that no one would think Barnabas and I drafted it alone. Syrian

Antioch had become our home base, and little could be more joyous than bringing good news home.

Syrian Antioch: Paul Confronts Peter

When we delivered the letter informing the primarily Gentile believers that strict adherence to Jewish law was not required for salvation, general celebration erupted. Those who had believed that circumcision and the Law were fundamental to salvation acted more subdued, but they, too, shared our joy at the new peace within the Church. We had handled this first major conflict and had come through in unity as the body of Christ. Together, we could move on.

Those who had traveled to Syrian Antioch with us returned home to Jerusalem while Barnabas and I stayed to teach and preach. But the decision we reached in Jerusalem, the decision that toppled the wall between the need-to circumcisers and the no-need-to circumcisers, also seemed to topple the wall between Jerusalem and Syrian Antioch. Before the decision, there had been an almost unconscious reluctance between the primarily Jewish Christians in Jerusalem and the primarily Gentile Christians in Antioch to engage in fellowship. Now, it seemed as if each side had been instilled with a curiosity about the other.

A few weeks after our return to Syrian Antioch, Peter arrived, joining us with a small group of believers from Jerusalem. I was never particularly close to Peter, but I couldn't help liking and even admiring him. He had an unassuming manner of kindness, never boisterous but always joyful. With such a personality, not to mention his reputation, he quickly and easily settled with us in Antioch as a long-lost friend. We prayed together, we laughed and sang together, and we ate together.

Then, Peter showed us how even someone as close to the Lord as he was still fallible. It happened several days later when more Jewish Christians that James had sent arrived from Jerusalem.

Just like the sinews of the body tie and hold it together, the Church as a whole needs something to tie and hold all the local churches together. There has to be something to keep an arm from flopping off on its own and doing damage to the body, but that something can't make salvation of the arm dependent on its behaving exactly like the leg. The local churches need to be bound in a unity but free to function in a way that best prepares its members to live lives in Christ.

Therefore, James had sent these men to start strengthening the tie between the Syrian Antioch church and the Jerusalem church. They had simply come as brothers and friends. But together with Peter, they almost cleaved the Church body in two again.

Even though we'd decided circumcision was unnecessary for salvation, even though we understood and accepted that Jews and Gentiles were equal under Christ, and even though we were all brothers, the Jewish believers whom James had sent separated themselves from the rest of the Antioch Church when it came time to eat so that they could maintain Jewish ritual purity. This probably wouldn't have been a big deal. The men knew each other well and didn't have any close relationships with Antioch believers. There was an air of exclusivity about them, but it seemed normal enough under the circumstances. The problem came when Peter abandoned the Antioch church to join them.

Peter is not a coward, but he does have a strong aversion to conflict. In his youth, he often wavered between chickening out and overreacting, forcing himself to do what he felt was the brave thing. He even cut off a Roman's ear in a fit of bravery one night only to deny knowing Jesus for fear of arrest the very next morning! Now, he has received the Holy Spirit, and he's grown far from the volatility of his youth. He follows the Holy Spirit and will do what he must, but he's the last person in the world to look for trouble, at least since I've known him.

Peter acted out of fear for the comfort of the Jewish believers from Jerusalem. He wanted everything to be all right all the time and acted to avoid conflict. What would these men think if he, a Jew by birth, ate with the Gentiles? Would they complain? Would the whole circumcision issue be relit? Better not risk it. So Peter separated himself from the rest of the congregation and ate with these men.

But the issue didn't stop at Peter and the men sent by James. When Peter separated himself, the rest of the Jewish Christians followed his lead, whether on impulse or intent. Even faithful Barnabas joined them.

A somber mood developed from the tension between the two groups. I don't know if the Jewish Christians felt superior in their propriety, but that was the general impression they gave to the

Gentile Christians. The rift threatened to rip into a great chasm, splitting the Church in two. Way to avoid conflict, brother.

As I looked at the two groups, trying to decide what to do, I noticed Titus. I had personally explained to this young man that he did not need to become Jewish to find salvation in the Lord. He had burned for the Lord with such brilliance that I had taken him under my wing. He made it a challenge for me to match his desire to grow in the Lord with my ability to teach. Now I saw him sit in dejection, feeling like an outsider. That was my snapping point.

And Peter—he was the linchpin for this split. He tied the Jewish Christians together, separating them from the Gentile Christians. This wasn't a matter of taking Peter or anyone else aside and quietly correcting them. The factious spirit had to be shattered! And to do so, I would rip out the linchpin. I have no problem with necessary confrontation.

I wheeled on the completely unsuspecting Peter: "Hey, Jew! You've lived like a Gentile from the time you arrived until these men arrived from Jerusalem. How can you now separate yourself with them?"

Peter sat bewildered and silent for a couple of seconds. I could see the broken start of a thought cross his face. "I don't expect... They don't have to..." But then he got it. Either they were the "real Christians," and everything we had decided in Jerusalem was hogwash, or they didn't belong as a separate group in their own little bubble.

I let him sit in awkward silence while he collected his thoughts. Then, surprisingly firmly, he said, "You're right." Turning his head to the Jewish Christians: "I'm sorry." He apologized simply but publicly for leading them astray, and picking up his meal, he walked over to join the Gentiles without another word.

Really, I'm very glad that Peter was the key to this situation. Settling this Antioch incident put into practice what had been decided in theory in Jerusalem. Who knows what would have happened if it had rested on the shoulders of someone less humble in nature or less open to the Holy Spirit than Peter? All differences aside, I do love him.

The confrontation with Peter highlighted the dangers of division, and shortly thereafter, I became agitated for the believers in the cities of my first missionary trip. More and more, I understood James's concern for some form of connection and unity between the local churches. I began to feel a great pressure, as if the young Christian communities of my first missionary journey would fall if I didn't rush out at once to strengthen them. Concern whipped my heart into a state of anxiety for our more remote, and still fledgling, brothers and sisters as the thorn in my side pricked me.

When I told Barnabas, he agreed with me: we should set out at once. But he wanted to take Mark with us. I didn't particularly dislike Mark, but I didn't really want him with us either. After all, he had started the last missionary trip with us but had bailed out before the real work had begun. He hadn't been with us in Iconium. He hadn't been with us when we were stoned in Lystra.

My jaw still catches and clicks when I try to open it all the way because of that pummeling.

I suppose that's all I need to say about the disagreement between Barnabas and me over Mark except to add that it did get fairly hot. In the end, neither Barnabas nor I would fold. Barnabas had fully committed to making another missionary trip, but he demanded Mark be allowed to accompany us. I, too, had fully committed to making another missionary trip, but my desire to be free of Mark was unshakable. I didn't care that they were cousins; we couldn't rely on Mark. We were quite angry with each other but more sorrowed by the obvious answer. The time had come for Barnabas and me to part ways, each of us leading our own mission.

I took the faithful brother Silas with me instead, along with Titus and a few others. We headed north, traveling over land through Syria for my second major tour, which we would make in the reverse order of my first tour. Meanwhile, Barnabas and Mark left for Cyprus in the same order of our first tour. Theoretically, we could cross paths with Barnabas and Mark, assuming Mark was going to stick it out this time.

Derbe and Lystra (Paul's Second Missionary Trip)

Our small team, at whose core were Silas, Titus, and me, began to grow straight away. In Lystra, we met Timothy, a young disciple who had earned a solid reputation with the Jews and Gentiles alike in the area. I talked to Silas about it, and he agreed that because Timothy was so highly esteemed, he might help bolster our credibility as we spread the gospel. We both thought

Timothy would make a great travel companion and fellow missionary. To our delight, he was eager to join us.

Unfortunately, Timothy's father was not a Jew, so he had not had Timothy circumcised. This wasn't a problem directly for Timothy or his salvation, of course, but we didn't want would-be listeners to blow off the gospel over such a superficial point of contention. Regardless of what we thought about the uselessness of circumcision, many Jews to whom we might try to testify would simply scoff at an uncircumcised Timothy.

Timothy didn't flinch when we cut into the subject with him. He agreed it was important the Jews didn't see faith in Christ as a simple invention of man, offering the one true God of the Jews without the attached hassle of Judaism. So, as an adult, Timothy decided to be circumcised. Timothy's circumcision highlighted his wisdom and willingness to sacrifice. It also made clear to Silas and me why he was so well respected. Ironically, part of the message we were delivering—along with the Gospel, of course—was the Jerusalem Council's decision that circumcision was unnecessary for salvation.

With the still-recovering Timothy now among our ranks, we helped to strengthen the churches we'd visited previously and added members to the faith every day. We worked our way through southern Turkey, heading north and west. But as we were heading north, the Holy Spirit stopped us. He did not let us continue into the far north of Turkey, so with the feel of that gentle hand blocking northward travel, we went to a port town in Turkey's extreme west.

While in this town, a vision came to me in the night. A man stood before me and told me to come to Macedonia to help the people there. It doesn't get much clearer than that. God had called us to preach the gospel in Macedonia, so off we went.

We set sail and landed about eight miles away from Philippi at the port closest to the city. Philippi, the main city in Macedonia, didn't have any Jewish presence to speak of, but we stayed there for some time.

On the Sabbath, we went out of the city gate and down to the river. We had assumed that the river would be a place of prayer, and we were right. We found some women there who had gathered for that purpose and preached the gospel to them. Here, a fairly wealthy merchant woman named Lydia had her heart opened to the Lord. We baptized her and her entire household.

Philippi: The Fortune-Telling Slave Girl

When we walked to the riverside place of prayer, we ran into a situation that even I'd never been in before. A slave girl met us along the way, but she wasn't exactly alone. She was possessed by a spirit that gave her the power of divination, or fortune-telling. She followed us around, crying out, "These men serve the highest God! They offer the way of salvation!"

As nice as having a trumpeter go before us may sound, I assure you that neither the girl nor the wicked spirit driving her had any intention of glorifying God or of helping us to spread His good news. This demon was manipulating its listeners into subconsciously clumping our Lord and Savior into a spiritual-philosophical-religious mishmash of ideas, theories, and practices. It was trying to make Jesus just another name among many. The demon seemed to admit that the Word was interesting by nature of its novelty, all the while carving the vague impression that Jesus wasn't beyond or above the world of sorcerers and fortune-tellers. I admit, the audacity of that conniving brute stoked my anger hot.

In this part of the world, there's money in fortune-telling, and this girl was accustomed to selling such a service. She knew how to turn a buck and had brought her owners big bucks. Our arrival had caused a bit of a stir in the city, and the slave girl saw our listeners as little piles of coins. The girl attached herself to us to serve her owners' pursuit of money and her demon's pursuit of wickedness.

She tagged along for days, trying to hitch her fortune-telling wagon to our team. I probably let her go on for too long. But finally, after days of her degrading behavior, I couldn't take it anymore. I looked her right in the face and commanded the spirit, "In the name of Jesus Christ, come out of her!" Within the hour, the spirit removed itself from the woman.

Though many people in Philippi had turned themselves over to the Way, we were still fighting an uphill battle. The majority perception of what I had done for the slave girl diverged significantly from the Truth: that I had freed the poor girl. As far as most people were concerned, I had not so much released her from that nasty, little spirit as I had taken the gift of fortune-telling away from her. Although the girl's owners had originally seen us as some type of circus with whom they could tag along for a little economic boost, they ended up losing all her earning potential. They were not happy with me, to say the least.

Arrested in Philippi

The slave girl's owners, furious over their loss, seized Silas and me and dragged us into the marketplace. They pushed us before the two Roman magistrates appointed to the colony, telling them we were Jews disturbing the peace by advocating things unlawful to Romans. It's funny how they didn't think we were disturbing the peace when they were making money off us.

The crowd joined the attack by shouting out affirmations of our guilt, so the magistrates had our clothes torn off and ordered us to be beaten with rods. Forget about a fair hearing; we didn't get to speak a word in our own defense. We took blow after blow after blow. And then, after the beating, we were thrown in prison, and stocks were placed on our feet.

Although I am honored to endure for the Lord, beatings do take their toll. I was very glad to have Silas with me this time. (Had Mark come, I imagine he would have returned home the previous day.) On the physical side, everything was dismal: unmitigated pain and discomfort. We were in prison, our feet in stocks, and our bodies aching. But on the spiritual side, Silas and I were both overwhelmed with joy.

Silas and I both had a strong sense that the unpleasant events of the day would ultimately benefit the growing Church. Our physical suffering completely quashed any endorphin-driven, good-times joy that anyone can experience from time to time.

But that deep-seated joy, the joy of knowing the Way, the joy that runs parallel to but separate from physical joy or pain, held our hearts and spirits high. So, in prison and in pain, our feet in stocks, we prayed and sang joyful hymns of praise to our great God.

Little did we know, there was a young physician sitting behind the jail who, listening to our songs, was experiencing that same joy for the first time. Luke had been quietly following on the fringes of our group for several days, making himself scarce at any sign of trouble. You can't blame him. Up until then, he had only been following out of a sense of curiosity. Luke will probably always be quiet, but he's also friendly, not remote or distant. For his quiet demeanor, he would prove no less steadfast for the Lord.

Silas and I prayed and sang until about midnight when there was a great earthquake that shook the prison right down to its foundation. During the earthquake, the doors flung open, and our bonds broke off. In the momentary chaos, I wasn't observant enough to notice if the earthquake had directly broken our bonds and blasted open the doors or if God had opened our confines separately from the quaking of the earth. Either way, only a fool wouldn't recognize this as a miracle.

Silas and I sat in awe of God as we looked from our freed feet to the gently swaying door. We were awestruck but not struck witless; we knew that God had opened the cell and broken our bonds. But Silas and I remained sitting silently. Without a word and without understanding why, there we sat, able to walk out but knowing that we were called to stay.

The jailer, whose name I'm embarrassed to admit I've forgotten, miraculously slept through the chaos. He awoke very shortly after the disturbance but not soon enough to have caught us if we'd made a break for it. We could've been long gone had God's will been for us to run.

When the jailer did wake, I couldn't tell if he was more shocked or upset at seeing the doors open. We could see him as he stood silhouetted against the doorframe, but he could not see us sitting in the darkness. He assumed that we had fled, so shame confronted him harshly, pushing him to suicide. (If we had escaped and he didn't commit suicide, he would have been accused of taking a bribe to let us go. This means the honorable man would have had to suffer intense shame AND probably be killed as punishment anyway.) He drew his sword for the task, but when I saw the blade, I shouted, "Stop! Don't do it! We're all here." He called for lights and then rushed in, shaking with fear and agitated nerves.

With fresh light from the new torches flooding the jail, exposing its inmates and their broken chains, the jailer collapsed before us. Then he brought us out of the prison and, with singular focus, asked what he had to do to be saved. Our remaining in the open prison had freed him of any doubt or skepticism about the Way, which he'd been listening to us sing about for hours before he'd fallen asleep. So we gave it to him in all its simplicity: "Believe in Jesus Christ the Lord."

When the jailer heard this, a flicker of joy flashed across his face. But it was almost instantly extinguished by a hard, duty-bound, stoic look. "Come," he more requested than commanded, and he led us off as though we marched for a military campaign with a clear objective. It wouldn't have surprised me if he had broken down in tears and professed his faith, nor could he have surprised me by reacting violently and beating me. But the unexplained determination in his demeanor perplexed me. We followed. Luke, still behind the prison, sat frozen, dazed in wonder.

Everything became clear when we reached our destination, the jailer's home, which was quite close to the prison. We *had* been marched on a mission. The duty-bound Roman, responsible not just for himself but for an entire household of people, had brought us to preach to all of them that they might be saved.

When we entered the house, the jailor ordered a servant to wake the household. The servant collected the family and the other servants as the jailor washed our wounds. Silas and I preached the Way of salvation in its simplest form, and everyone present believed, so we baptized his entire household.

The jailor's baptism washed the remaining stoicism from his face. He was saved, and he had done his duty to his household that they, too, might find salvation. Rejoicing now permeated the entire household, and smiling servants brought us food.

Of course, we returned to prison before the morning light and waited until the magistrates sent for our release. We half expected the release order to come without trial, and come it did. We hadn't done anything wrong, and there was no reason for our arrests in the first place, so the magistrate wanted to quietly let us go. But when a new jailer on the morning shift came to set us free, I told him that we would not leave. After all, I was a Roman citizen entitled to the protections of the Roman law. But they had beaten me publicly and thrown me into prison without a proper trial, so I wasn't going to let them secretly throw me out after putting me there with such a public display.

When the message of my stance was delivered to the magistrates, and they learned of my Roman citizenship, they were afraid. Had I been just another Jew without Roman citizenship, as they had assumed, no one would have cared. But because I was a Roman citizen, I had special rights. They knew they could be held accountable to higher Roman authorities for their actions against me. My pride didn't need an apology, but putting them in the hot seat now might later cause them to hesitate before acting so flippantly with their power. Driven by fear, the magistrates came personally to the prison to release us. They apologized up and down to us for our treatment but did ask us to leave the city to keep the atmosphere from boiling over again. With this apology, we gladly obliged. *Hasta la vista*, baby.

Thessalonica

After passing through some smaller towns, we made it to Thessalonica, which was still in northern Greece. As usual, we started by trying our luck in the synagogue. I've always thought of my fellow Jews as a very reasonable, logic-minded people, and I certainly thought of myself that way. Every time I entered a synagogue, I expected this assumption to work in our favor. After all, the Way of Christ, once revealed, is the obvious outcome of the Scriptures. Even setting revelation aside, it's logically consistent with Scripture.

In every synagogue I spoke in, I built a bridge of reason leading toward salvation. For three Sabbaths, I preached in the Thessalonian synagogue. I was allotted much time to speak because the Thessalonian Jews could see that bridge and followed me far across it. The trouble was that I could never, and will never be able to, finish the bridge so it reaches salvation. No matter how long, wide, or solidly I built, the bridge always ended before it reached that perfect destination. From the edge of the bridge, one ultimately must be willing to make the leap of faith to reach the far shore.

So, after three weeks, the bridge was as solid as I could build it. Some Jews had jumped to the salvation shore and experienced the joy and beauty that they never could have seen had they remained on the bridge. The more stubborn of the Jews, of course, never set foot on the bridge at all. But after three weeks, most stood there awkwardly, all the way out on the edge of the bridge, unwilling to jump. They had followed the logic of the Scriptures as I spoke and understood the necessity of Christ's suffering, His death, and His resurrection, but to jump was another thing entirely. They quietly backed away from the edge of the bridge, backtracking on the sound logic they themselves had followed, hoping to avoid the embarrassment of being seen on the bridge at all. And after three weeks, we could gain no more ground at the synagogue.

After three Sabbaths attending synagogue, we remained in Thessalonica, during which time the Gentiles proved much more willing to make the leap of faith. I was familiar enough with the Greek world, but by no means did my understanding of it match my Pharisee-background intimacy with Judaism. The bridge of reason I built for the Greeks, a much shakier bridge than that I had made for the Jews, was walked by throngs of Greeks. And when they reached the edge, many more of them jumped for their salvation.

Our numbers swelled in Thessalonica primarily from the new Greek believers. The Jews watched the Greeks flood to the Way and saw the joy they experienced at finding salvation. They grew jealous, and probably a bit embarrassed, for having flirted with the Way only to ultimately turn from it. Plus, drawing converts in Thessalonica was, in a way, encroaching upon their turf. But jealousy doesn't need much reason; the most jealous and wicked among them collected as a small group. This small group, however, worked up excitement in others and slowly festered into an all-out, angst-driven mob.

The thoughtless mob stormed the house where we were staying, planning to drag me off. We weren't there, but the attackers didn't turn to hunt for Silas and me elsewhere. They settled for grabbing Jason, the homeowner and our host, along with some other believers, and dragged them off to the Roman city authorities.

They told the authorities that Silas and I were the men who had flipped the world upside down and that Jason had taken us in and given us aid. They told the authorities that we acted against the decrees of Caesar and proclaimed Jesus as a competing king. The people and authorities were really startled by these charges. Of course, the authorities might have been somewhat relieved had they given Jason a chance to defend himself.

The authorities took money from Jason and the others as a type of bail. The money was security that would be forfeit if Silas and I continued to "disturb the peace." My refusal to stop preaching the gospel, combined with a post-riot atmosphere, left little chance of continued success. We assumed our friends' money was gone. Popular cynicism warned that the authorities never returned money once confiscated from Jews. But as we could do little more in Thessalonica than whip up riot, there remained no practical reason to stay. Our Thessalonian brothers sent us off that night.

Out of Thessalonica

Having been forced out of Thessalonica, we went to the neighboring town of Berea. Here, the Jews were more open-minded. We preached the gospel daily, and they listened. They paid close attention and examined our every word against the Scriptures. And, as always, sound logic and reason supported our preaching. With this group of Jews, however, the emotional resistance to change proved less a hindrance than in Thessalonica. Desire for Truth urged many to leap to Christ.

Unfortunately, the Jews from Thessalonica were not satisfied with our exile from their city. When they learned that we were preaching in Berea, they came and began trying to rile up the crowd. (I know. *Déjà vu*, right?) But this time, we didn't let it get as out of hand as in Thessalonica. I, quietly but openly, left town without getting stoned. Some brothers accompanied me as far as Athens, but Silas and Timothy stayed behind.

In this case, we acted too hastily on our resolution to preserve the peace. In the big picture, we made the right decision, but we should have planned the details more thoroughly. My name had stirred the most trouble, so the necessity of my swift departure spurred the decision that I also split from Timothy and Silas, taking just a few companions with me.

By the time I made it to Athens, I realized parting had been a mistake. We'd barely stumbled into the famous city before I sent my companions back to tell Timothy and Silas to come join me in Athens as soon as possible.

Athens

While I waited for Timothy and Silas, I preached not only in the synagogue but also in the marketplace and everywhere else I found ears, for that matter. All the creepy, empty idols in Athens served at least one good purpose: they inspired me to crank it up a notch and pour even more energy into preaching the gospel. Plus, on the more positive side, the plethora of idols was clear evidence of the people's groping for God, though without success. They even had an altar in honor of the, evidently worth honoring, "Unknown God," for crying out loud.

In Athens, I debated with Epicurean and Stoic philosophers, among others. And I had thought the Jews were stubborn! While these philosophers held themselves as great thinkers open to reason, they weren't any more ready for new ideas than the Jews of Jerusalem. They made huge leaps to bridge the gaps of logic in their own preconceived notions and called me a babbler for my lack of intellectual athleticism. Their starting point seemed to have been that there was no god, or no god of the Jews, or that the Jews overemphasized the greatness of their god. Having fully rejected the Scriptures, there was no amount of logic or any other tool I could use to bring them to Christ.

On the other hand, they did love to hear new things. This was more of a love for novelty or fairy tales than a real willingness to hear the Word of the Lord. Still, I was allowed to talk about my "new teachings" in the famous Areopagus of Athens. With the ears of many tuned to me, I played the philosopher:

"You Athenians are very religious people," I told them. "Walking through town, I've seen the objects that you worship. You even have an altar dedicated to the unknown god."

I didn't want to be overtly rude, but I did want them to consider how silly their completely unfocused worship was. It was as if they groped for anything decent to worship but found nothing. Were they to accept the gospel, they could brush all that useless distraction aside and hold to salvation.

Thus, having pointed to their worship of petty idols, I proclaimed the God of All Creation, the Lord of Heaven and Earth to them. "God is not like your man-made temple trinkets that need you to serve them. He is the One who gives to us! He gives us everything: life, breath, everything! God made every nation from one man. God determines how long the nations live and their boundaries. God's purpose in creating us was that we might feel our way to Him. God is not far from any of us, if only we seek Him." As offensive as some of them might have found this monotheism, I didn't shrink from the Truth.

I expected that this address to the Areopagus would be my best opportunity in Athens, so I gave it my all. I even quoted their pagan writers, hoping it would make them more at ease with the message I preached. All the while, I hammered home the fact that God is not some little, man-made trinket of metal, stone, or wood. I called on them to repent and turn to God.

When I had finished speaking, some people mocked me, especially about the resurrection of the dead. But some believed and joined me as I left them. Others were left on the fence, but they said they would hear me again. I supposed they were the type of people who would have responded the same way to anyone's message, the type who live on the fence. It was clear that there was little left to be accomplished in Athens, so I moved on without waiting for Timothy and Silas. I'm afraid that to most Athenians, God would remain unknown.

Corinth: First Visit and Planting the Church

With Athens not being a wild success but not falling into riotous violence either, I started the forty-six-mile trek to Corinth. The southern end of Greece is almost an island, but it's connected to the rest of Greece by a narrow passage of land only four miles wide. Corinth is a couple of miles in from this isthmus to the west of the would-be island, but it basically has control of the passage. This means Corinth has two ports to send and receive sea traffic from, one on each side of the isthmus.

Another interesting feature of Corinth is the favor it has with Rome. About two hundred years before I visited Corinth, Rome was victoriously wrapping up its war with Carthage and its wars with the Greek cities to become the undisputed empire champion. At this time, Corinth was wiped out—gone. About one hundred years before my visit, the city was reborn when Rome settled people here as a Roman colony. Roman favor and being ideally situated for commerce have turned Corinth into a booming place; it's the most powerful and influential city in southern Greece. While the culture, gods, and sexual immorality of Corinth are still largely Roman, these things have all been supplemented by people from around our world brought in by trade and big city draw.

Soon after I arrived in Corinth, I met a man named Aquila. He had been forced out of Rome by then-Emperor Claudius's decree banning all Jews, including Jewish Christians, from the city *(about AD 49)*. Many Jewish Christians like Aquila moved to Corinth.

In Corinth, I stayed with Aquila. Because we were both tentmakers, I got a job working with him. My self-support, not to mention my willingness to take abuse, proved that, for all the horrible things people have said about my sanity, no reasonable person could claim that I preached for an ulterior motive. But the Corinthians remained shockingly skeptical, suspecting me of scamming them for cash.

Silas and Timothy caught up with me in Corinth, where I was preaching in the synagogue every Sabbath until it was clear I had, once again, hit a brick wall. The Jews opposed and reviled me at every turn. Having seen it all before, I symbolically shook out my garments and loudly announced that their blood was on their own heads. I had done everything I could to bring the

Jews to Christ. Now, having also satisfied my flair for the dramatic, I turned to the Gentiles.

Much to the dismay of many of the Corinthian Jews, I didn't go far. I wound up teaching the Word at a believer's house, right next door to the synagogue. Titus Justus (*not the Titus who spent time traveling with Paul and to whom Paul wrote the biblical letter*) was a new believer. But he was on fire to spread the Word, so he eagerly invited me to preach in his home when I left the synagogue in a bit of a huff.

Not all the Corinthian Jews held out, obstinate against the Lord. The ruler of the synagogue and his household came to have faith in Christ, which was a surprising score. And many Gentile Corinthians believed, turned to Christ, and were baptized. In fact, so many people in Corinth came to the Way that Titus Justus's house seemed to shrink in around us over time until we found a more suitable meeting place.

In Corinth, the Lord came to me in a vision and told me not to be afraid but to go on speaking and preaching the Word. He told me that He was with me and that I would be safe because many of the Corinthians were His people.

I would face any challenge at the Lord's command, but this vision gave me great comfort. After being forced from so many places by violence, I was able to stay right there in Corinth, teaching the Word of God without concern for a year and a half. Also, knowing that many Corinthians were the Lord's was very comforting during those yet-to-come hard times when the Corinthian church fell into rampant sin.

Before my time in Corinth ended, however, the Jews brought yet another attack against me. I'd had a good run, a year and a half, so I couldn't complain. They took me before the Roman proconsul for judgment, saying I was persuading people to worship God contrary to Roman law. But before I could speak, the proconsul kicked us out of his court. He said it was up to the Jews to settle the matter amongst ourselves. Officially, it was a matter only involving Jewish law and not crime against Roman law. Practically, they had absurdly trumped up this charge to a crime against Rome, but they should have known that the Roman proconsul wouldn't want to deal with it.

It was nice to have it spelled out clearly: Christianity does not infringe upon Roman law. There wasn't much time for celebration, however. The Jews were enraged that I had escaped punishment. They focused their anger on the ruler of the synagogue. They blamed him for making a procedural error by taking me before the proconsul instead of inflicting harsh punishment directly. They grabbed him and thoroughly beat him right there as the Roman proconsul watched from the doorway. The proconsul, for his part, paid the attack as much attention as he had paid to my case—none.

Returning to Syrian Antioch

I stayed in Corinth for eighteen months before heading to Syrian Antioch. Aquila and Priscilla, his wife, accompanied me. Once we made it to Corinth's eastern port, I cut my hair because I had completed the terms of a vow I had made earlier. (I'm not going to discuss the vow because I don't want to romanticize it or otherwise encourage Christians to make vows. Vows are completely unnecessary under Christ, and they inflict much responsibility and consequence upon the person proclaiming them.) Then we sailed to Ephesus, where I left Aquila and Priscilla.

As it turned out, leaving them in Ephesus brought a much bigger return for the Kingdom of God than I could have ever hoped for. While they were there, a man named Apollos came to the city. He was on fire with the Spirit, and he taught enthusiastically about Jesus. He had a powerful base of scriptural knowledge, but his knowledge about Jesus was limited to the baptism of John.

Apollos's story makes me think back to my early years as a Christian, and I blush a little when I consider how much I ran my mouth on such limited knowledge. Still, every Christian is duty-bound to spread the gospel to the best of his or her ability. Those who always learn but never teach are failing in their Christian mission to bring others into the Way.

Aquila and Priscilla heard Apollos speak boldly in the synagogue and were impressed, even though he fell short on knowledge. They quietly took him aside after the service and provided him with a much-needed education, and he became a great mouthpiece for the Word. We sent Apollos to Corinth, where he refuted the Jews by using Scripture to show that Jesus is the Christ.

Before I left Ephesus, I stopped in at the local synagogue to proclaim the gospel, but my stay in town was more of a pit stop on my way home. Declining an invitation to stay longer, I sailed to Caesarea, the closest port city to Antioch and Jerusalem. I greeted the church members there but didn't linger before finishing my trip and settling back in Syrian Antioch.

CHAPTER 3:

Third Missionary Trip

Ephesus: News from Corinth

(Paul has a habit of stating "I this" or "I that" when he was, in fact, part of a larger group. Paul being the leader, this should be seen as taking responsibility for the group and not as an attempt to hog the spotlight.)

In the spring, I launched my third major tour, with Luke this time. We started traveling through Turkey again, strengthening the disciples in those regions. This time, the Holy Spirit did not hinder my travels, so I made my way back to Ephesus over land. I had many close relationships in the church at Ephesus, so I had plenty of pleasant company. And again, I stayed with my closest friends, Aquila and Priscilla.

Priscilla and Aquila gave me a hint of news about Corinth. (Corinth is on mainland Greece, and Ephesus is on the west coast of Turkey, separated by the Aegean Sea; you can get from one to the other by boat or over land by going around the sea.) They had been in regular contact via letter with Apollos, whom we'd stationed in Corinth. They mentioned a problem with division and strife at Corinth but said Apollos could give a better account, and I left it at that.

A couple of days later, Apollos arrived in Ephesus. I embarrassed myself by asking how he'd heard I was there. My assumption was that he sought my wisdom as a mentor. As it turned out, divine coincidence had brought us to Ephesus at the same time.

When the Corinthian situation, the full extent of which I wasn't yet aware, had escalated, Apollos left because he felt his presence was doing more harm than good. He departed the ostentatious Greek city and came to the ostentatious Turkish city where he planned on collecting his wits and then deciding what to do about Corinth. (It does help to have one's wits together when planning.) I helped Apollos settle in at Aquila and Priscilla's and waited until the next day to press him about Corinth.

The Corinthian situation was this: Corinth was almost a mini-Rome but even more cosmopolitan per capita (if you can say that). The city nurtured any vice or virtue that one cared to have nurtured. Of course, many Corinthians and visitors to the city gave preferential nurturing to those fleshly vices. The sex industry in Corinth was booming, and it was a source of attraction for the city. Back in old Corinth, over two hundred years ago, before the Romans wiped it out, Aphrodite's Temple on the mountain that overlooks the city was a busy place; a thousand temple prostitutes worked there.

The new city of Corinth, as rebuilt by the Romans one hundred years ago, doesn't hit the same mark of depravity, but they aim for it and boast of their "glorious" past. This atmosphere choked the seedling of the Corinthian church. And here is the tightrope for a church leader caring for Corinth: on one hand, the Corinthian Christians are babies in the Way and need soft coddling. Though some are strong, most struggle to break their drive for physical pleasures. They must be dealt with in all love and understanding. On the other hand, sexual immorality and pornographic behavior are not to be tolerated in the Church.

To these people who see orgies as a socially acceptable and common form of a get-together, we have to convey that sexual license is morally wrong and against God's will. Of equal importance, we have to consider how the outside world perceives the Church. We cannot give the impression that morally debased behavior is something Christians can turn a blind eye to.

Apollos explained how the various weeds of sin had proliferated in Corinth and were overtaking the seedling church. Even when I had left, the stability of the moral behavior of the believers in Corinth was questionable at best. Now, Apollos informed me that if it deteriorated any further, the church would collapse. The believers at Corinth fought and bickered over everything from earthly grievances to theological questions. And, worst of all, they had all but broken into sects based on the Church leader they claimed to follow.

When I had left Corinth a year and a half earlier, I understood they were not well-established or strong in the Word. So I wrote a letter to them from Antioch to encourage and strengthen them. (*This letter, now lost, was written before 1 Corinthians of the New Testament.*)

I may have shown too much haste with the letter. Of course, it addressed sexual morality, but it also briefly touched on Christian freedom from the Law, and it was written softly, as I feared harsher language may have broken the Corinthians down when I really wanted to build them up.

Apollos now informed me that the Corinthians had widely misunderstood and misused my letter. Even those who claimed, "I follow Paul," used the letter to bolster their position and didn't fare any better with the contents than the rest of the congregation. Many—and this must have been willful if you consider the rest of the letter—misinterpreted Christian freedom as freedom from morality. They became open and unashamed of their most licentious and wild sexual behavior. One of them had open sexual relations with his stepmother, something that even many pagans find morally disturbing. Many of the congregation just shrugged their shoulders at such behavior. On the other side of the coin, unmarried believers who accepted celibacy claimed a position of superiority to married believers who had sex with their spouses.

In short, the letter was a monumental flop and a failure. I'd told the Lord I couldn't handle this commission! The thorn was driving hard into my side as Apollos spoke. As I listened to his explanation, it became clear that factionalism was the biggest problem, though pride and arrogance caused the factionalism. The Corinthians had queued up with their preferred Church leader and all but completely neglected Christ. Some announced that they followed Apollos, others Peter, and others still proclaimed to follow me. The handful that put on airs of rising above the factionalism claimed, "I follow Jesus," but that seemed only to mean that they followed their own will.

All the disputes either came from or fueled this factionalism. For example, I'm not married and have no interest in such a distraction. Peter, who is softer—and I'm only stating the facts—is married and visited Corinth with his wife. Thus, even the legitimate question, "Should I get married?" might hide the danger of a Peter-Paul factional conflict.

As usually happens with such factionalism, the Corinthians weren't content to support their favorite alone. They felt compelled to sling mud at the competition, so there were a lot of nasty and untrue things being said of me. What's worse, there were a lot of nasty and untrue things being said of Peter and Apollos in my name.

The community had broken down. The atmosphere, as I was told, had become more like an unhappy carnival. Individual groups of people would take their own food and drink and stuff themselves and even get drunk while those who were hungry, right next to them, could only watch.

I can't imagine how frustrating this must have been for Apollos, who had been right there teaching that we are only Church leaders, ministering the Word for Christ. He worked desperately to break the division, but the Corinthians continued proclaiming his name, bolstering the Adversary's message of faction.

Receiving this message put me ill at ease. I had been eager for a day of joyful reunion with my friends in Ephesus, but now

I was so distraught that I could hardly pay attention to anything Aquila and Priscilla had to say. I tried to be sociable with my friends, but they understood my state and acted with grace. Quite early, they began apologizing for being exhausted and begged my forgiveness if they retired early, mercifully letting me go to bed in my heavy melancholy. But before departing, Aquila quietly approached me, handed me a folded letter from a group of Corinthians, and said, "There is still hope for Corinth. They, or at least many of them, still want to know. They want to follow the Way set out by the Lord."

At this point, the letter was such a surprise that it simply didn't cross my mind to be annoyed with Aquila for waiting so long to give it to me. Normally, I like to be the one in charge and don't like to be played with like this. But when I realized what he had done, I had to admit that Aquila had been wise not to give me the letter when its hope would have been swallowed up in empty frustration. I work with great people and might need to appreciate their judgment more.

The letter was poorly composed, no more than a list of questions, and theologically childish questions at that. But it heartened me to see such earnestness penned by the believers. They did want to strengthen their faith and go deeper into the Way. I lay in bed that night, turning the letter over in my mind. Their letter helped me walk in their shoes, and I spent what felt like hours considering how I could best help them before sleep overtook me.

The next day, I awoke feeling more positive but frantic about helping the Corinthians. I talked to Timothy and Apollos about sending them to Corinth to work for the restoration of the church. Apollos flatly refused. He was as respectful as possible, but getting him back in that ring was clearly off the table. He explained that his being in Corinth as an unwilling leader of a faction, not to mention the difficulty he had displaying love under those conditions, would render his services in that city useless. But he didn't tell me this to open the matter up for discussion. I had to accept that he wasn't returning to Corinth anytime soon. Ultimately, he was probably right.

Timothy, though, had not burned out trying to guide the Corinthians, and his heart grieved deeply for them. It didn't please him to leave Ephesus so quickly, but he was eager to do all he could for Corinth. We called the brothers and sisters in Christ together and spent the rest of the morning in prayer. That afternoon, Timothy was on a ship that would land him in Corinth after only a couple of stops.

I had expected Timothy's departure to put me more at ease. Apollos had described a bad situation. We all accepted this as true and were genuinely concerned. But when I thought about Corinth, I still thought of the people, the community, and the overall joy I had sailed away from after that eighteen-month stay when I founded the church. Plus, they were all already Christians. How hard could it really be to give them a little loving redirection? I expected Timothy to return in no time at all. Still, discomfort ate at me.

The rest of the day trapped us in an awkward state in which we couldn't escape talking about Corinth even though we'd long run out of things to say on the topic. I don't know how many times Aquila said, "It's just that… It's just that I don't see how they can claim to follow Apollos when Apollos was right there telling them that they are to follow the Christ, not humans. I mean, it's… It's not just wrong to follow Apollos as a sect, but if they're not even listening to him, how can they say they're following him?" And that's how the conversation sputtered around until we made a conscious effort to break for a few hours of prayer before bed.

After we had been praying for some time, the thorn pricked sharply in my side. Guided by the Holy Spirit, I knew my next step. I told Sosthenes, one of the disciples on our team who had been acting as my scribe, "Break out your pen and paper. I need you to take a letter for me." And I sat down to dictate another letter for the Corinthians. (*This letter became 1 Corinthians in the New Testament.*)

Sosthenes had heard there was a ship sailing directly to Corinth late the next afternoon, but he wasn't clear on the specifics. We would try to have him on that ship.

The letter was long. My main point was to break this disunity and pull the church back together again. I covered that as thoroughly as possible. But then a dam broke, and I flooded the letter with everything I felt I needed to say to the Corinthians. Misuse of my earlier letter had to stop, for one. But I also wanted to address the theological concerns the believers had written to me about. I softened the letter with kind and truthful words about my love for them, but there was no hiding the overall harshness of the letter, written to spell everything out with crystal clarity lest the Corinthians misuse it.

The Corinthians needed to understand that sexual immorality was off the table for Christians. It's not up to us to judge non-Christians, but within the Church, we must purge the evil. Because God dwells within us, our bodies are his temple. Thus, defiling yourself is to defile God's temple when you should be glorifying it. The Corinthian church needed to kick out those who defiled their temples. If they were allowed to remain comfortably within the church, as everyone turned a blind eye, what incentive would they have to repent and behave more in accord with God's will?

Early the next morning, I sent Sosthenes to the docks to inquire about that ship traveling to Corinth. I expected him to return within the hour, but the sun had peaked and started its retreat, and we still had no word from him. I found him at the docks, sweating profusely and loading large sacks of grain onto a ship.

"Can't talk long," he said, out of breath. "This ship sails directly to Corinth as soon as it's loaded. The captain will carry me without a fee. But I must work with the crew, loading here and unloading there." I wished him safe travels and then let him perform his duty to the captain.

Forcing myself to leave the Corinthian situation up to the letter Sosthenes carried and get back into my groove, I went to the synagogue to exercise some of that good, old-fashioned, bold speech and reasoning with the Jews. Considering my luck at some of the other places I'd been, I suppose I had a good run this time, but it did come to an end. When some of the Jews grew more stubborn, continuing in unbelief and speaking evil about the gospel, I discontinued my teaching there. Instead, I took the few who did believe with me to Aquila and Priscilla's house.

Ephesus: Some Baptized Only into the Baptism of John

About a dozen faithful men I met in Ephesus startled me considerably when they told me that not only had they not received the Holy Spirit, but that they hadn't even heard of Him. They had not received the baptism of Christ but had been baptized into that of John the Baptist.

I explained to them that John's baptism was of repentance and that the "one to come after" John was Jesus. This excited the men, pumping them full of joy, and I baptized them in the name of the Lord Jesus. I placed my hands on them, and the Holy Spirit came on them, and they spoke in tongues and prophesied.

This hadn't been the only time I had met people baptized into the baptism of John who did not know about Jesus. Initially, I found it very disturbing that this sect of Jews who followed John seemed to have developed. Here was another Scripture-based and technically accurate but not complete group to deal with. But upon baptizing these Ephesians in the baptism of the Christ, I realized that the work of John still bore fruit. These people had been perfectly prepared to receive the Word of the Lord. And when they received the gospel, they all faithfully leapt for their salvation and were eager to be baptized in the baptism of Jesus. I got the impression that John the Baptist had led flocks to the edge of the bridge to salvation. But unlike the majority of Jews, they stood on the edge, waiting eagerly for the opportunity to jump to their salvation. They simply needed someone to tell them the jump was possible.

John the Baptist wasn't a little blip in the Scriptures. He truly helped prepare the way for Christ, almost as a pre-apostle whose work still bore fruit!

Ephesus: Seven Sons of Sceva

God has done extraordinary things through my hands. When a handkerchief or an apron touched my skin and then was carried off to a sick person, an evil spirit was purged from that person, and the disease fled their body.

As the people had been accustomed to soothsayers, fortune-tellers, and magicians, they didn't always understand that these miracles weren't some mysterious powers I had conjured up. I didn't make magic hankies. It was the power of the Lord God working through faith in Jesus Christ. I was merely an instrument. But through this misunderstanding, the seven sons of Sceva blundered.

The Jewish high priest named Sceva had seven sons. I don't know if they had witnessed the Lord heal the sick or drive out demons through my hands or if they had only heard of these incidents. Either way, they didn't at all understand; they thought I was whipping some sort of power around simply by saying, "In the name of Jesus." They thought it was cool, so they decided to see what their own hands could do. After all, they knew the magic words.

There was a man known to be driven by a spirit of violence. With no faith in Jesus Christ but probably feeling secure in their number, the seven brothers determined that they would overcome the demon and cast it from the man. They tried to invoke the name of Jesus, and even my name. After closing themselves up in a house with the superhumanly strong psychopath, they tried giving orders to the demon.

"Get out! Get out of that man! In the name of Jesus, whom Paul talks about, get out!" they commanded.

But the evil spirit felt only gleeful amusement as it pushed the possessed man's face into a sneer. "I know Jesus, and I know His Paul," it said. "But who are you to me?"

Any confidence or self-induced sense of power the men had had fled them; each and all were overcome with fear and then overcome by the wicked spirit. The man, with the evil spirit driving him, leapt on them. He overpowered and mastered them—all seven of them—so that they fled the house naked, beaten, and suffering intense shame.

This story, driven by all its dramatic elements and gruesome details, flew over the land, becoming widely known to the Jews and Gentiles of Ephesus and beyond. It was a harsh lesson for the brothers to learn, but as the story spread so, too, did the lesson. The benefit was great and to a great many people. If anyone who heard the story had trouble with theoretical concepts, this story helped spell it out for them. I was no powerful magician, capable of conjuring up the power of God. Rather, God chose to use his great power through my otherwise powerless hands.

This understanding brought a healthy fear to many, and they celebrated the name of the Lord Jesus.

News of the seven sons of Sceva convinced many to turn to Jesus, that is, to truly turn over their hearts and not just passively or intellectually assent to His greatness. They came in throngs to me and the other mature Christians in Ephesus to confess their sins and practices. Many of them had practiced magic in the past, and they brought their wicked magic books and burned them in the presence of all. This was not a few books, either. The blaze consumed a total value of about 50,000 pieces of silver.

I have to admit mild amusement from looking at those fresh Christian faces in the light of the great blaze. I couldn't help but think that such a bonfire would have had them dancing and chanting a week previously. This great, dramatic, mass conversion seemed to have a snowballing effect of adding to the story of the seven sons of Sceva so that more and more people came to Christ.

Ephesus: Timothy and Sosthenes Return

I hadn't planned very well with Sosthenes when he left, and I had no idea when to expect his return. I wasn't sure if he was dropping the letter off and coming straight back or if he was going to settle in at Corinth with Timothy for a while. But summer had passed, and the cooler weather of autumn had come before Sosthenes and Timothy returned. They looked like dejected soldiers bringing bad news to their sergeant.

The news was bad. The Corinthians themselves had written to me to ask about order in the church and how to deal with people who speak in tongues and people who prophesy. Just from their mention of these subjects, I could tell they were having trouble keeping orderly service. My reply letter that Sosthenes had delivered *(1 Corinthians)* detailed how they should not despise those who speak in tongues, which is a gift from the Holy Spirit, but it also explained that these people should not be given prominence. What good does it do for the church to listen to babble?

Timothy explained how the Corinthian church even failed to provide basic instruction in doctrine to combat the false doctrine floating amongst them because it could not function as a single unit. These people were so often whipped up into an ecstasy and speaking in tongues that they would jump up randomly and often: whooping, hollering, and proclaiming no-one-knows-what. Small groups of the faithful would break off to pray together or study Scripture to see how Jesus fit in, but nothing could be done as a congregation.

Timothy explained how my letter impacted the factions within the Corinthian church in different ways. The faithful, who made up only a fraction of the church, had eagerly accepted my letter and begun a campaign to pull the church together. This group seemed to have been comprised of the most mature believers of all the factions, not just of those who "followed Paul."

But what could this minority do against such a riot? The speakers of tongues didn't want to settle down and control themselves. (Though I should state that not all with the gift acted inappropriately.) And no one wanted the uncomfortable task of confronting their friends about sexually inappropriate behavior. My letter seemed to have been rocky ground that was about to land the Corinthian ship, whether safely or by smashing it to pieces.

The faithful in Corinth could pull the church together; I knew they could do it. But even Timothy was still quite new as a leader, and now they didn't even have him. They needed guidance, and this was my commission. So many doors for spreading the gospel seemed wide open right there. There seemed so much untapped potential in Asia from Ephesus, but I couldn't venture out to bring more people into the Way, knowing I would be sacrificing Corinth.

It all boiled down to my commission from the Lord. I was to establish the Church in His name. That meant bringing people into the Way, keeping people in the Way, and strengthening people in the Way. My duty was to do everything in my power to bring Corinth to a safe landing, establish it as a place of orderly worship, and make it a center of moral behavior.

Another ship wasn't to leave for Corinth for a few days, but when it did, Timothy and I were on it. I was excited to know I was doing what I must, and Timothy was encouraged to return at my side. (Sosthenes excused himself with a vague claim that he had business in Ephesus and found the understanding company of Apollos.)

Corinth: The Painful Visit

As the ship came into port, my spirits were higher than ever. I was ready to rush into the blazing fire to save my child! But Timothy's face had fallen. When he noticed me looking at him, he smiled broadly in encouragement, but he couldn't hide his apprehension. I got the impression that he, too, envisioned us rushing into an inferno-ravaged building to save a baby, but he seemed more aware of how badly burns hurt.

I quickly shook off the uneasiness Timothy's demeanor had transferred to me. He was young and suffering shell shock from his first visit. I was not only established in the Church, but I was also a long-established establisher of churches. I'd just had three days at sea to collect my thoughts and prepare for Corinth; it was time to swoop in and wrap up what the others couldn't quite handle.

We arrived on a beautiful autumn day. I'd right everything at the church meeting the next day, and, assuming a ship to take us, we'd be back off to Ephesus the day following that. Now it was time to settle and enjoy the day with friends and food. After our wobbly, just-off-the-boat walk to Stephenas's house, we knocked on the door. I was still beaming with enthusiasm. Timothy looked down and away from the door.

When Stephenas's servant opened the door, his "It's good to see you" didn't match the look on his face. He led us in, seated us, and then solemnly went to retrieve his master as if bearing terrible news.

When Stephenas joined us, he did a much better job appearing joyful than the others, but I could tell that he, too, wasn't completely comfortable. My existence in Corinth seemed to unnerve everyone I was close to. Still, completely avoiding any discussion about the church, we had a nice time together. The servants brought some cakes as well as wine mixed with water, but Timothy would only drink plain water as he never drank wine. The mood lifted as we silently agreed not to discuss serious matters. And what of them? I had the Corinthian matter all sorted in my head and would square everything away tomorrow.

The next morning, we headed to the meeting place, which was in an old warehouse by the docks. It was farther up and in a poor location for loading its stores onto the ships. Its owner had made more money by making a couple of modifications and renting it out to the less prosperous classes of Corinth for special events. When he turned to the Way, he offered it up as a place of meeting for the Corinthian Christians. As so many Corinthians had turned to the Way, the larger space was much needed and welcome.

When the warehouse came into sight, I was staggered by the scene. People were everywhere. The huge warehouse doors were wide open, and people appeared to spill out. One man even performed tricks off to the side of the throng as if at a circus.

People yelled loudly to the crowd in languages no one understood. But as I listened, I heard the consistency of characters and melody of a real, though unknown, language. They weren't frauds; they were worshiping the Lord.

No sooner had I taken in this sight than we heard loud singing from inside the warehouse and then a banging rhythm as accompaniment. The singer broke forth from the doors, followed by the drummer and a host of dancers. The song and dance were of joy, offered up in praise to the Lord. The large group trailed the singer, flowing this way and that like a river that couldn't find its course.

Timothy looked uncomfortable, and Stephenas actually looked ashamed. But I'd been shocked into wonder at the huge number of people and their outwardly joyful praise to the Lord. So what if the joy was a little messy? After a moment of closer observation, though, my vision cleared. I saw the messenger of Satan in the local church. I felt the twisting thorn in my side. The church in Corinth had grown at an unprecedented rate but wildly and without any willingness to grow in a managed direction.

I noticed the singer intentionally bump into another man who had been quietly reading in a group. The interrupted man looked up, scowling, to see the singer sneer back at him. I watched a woman loudly bleating who-knows-what in the unknown language. But now, I noticed her tendency to tilt her head to the left when she trumpeted her words. If she turned to the right, it was only for a second to give the appearance of speaking to all. But then she would turn to the left and blare out much louder than she had in the other direction. She was trying to drown out the voices of the prophets in the next group. They wouldn't have been too productive even if she hadn't been there, though. A small scuffle broke out among the group that had been prophesying. Apparently, they hadn't learned to take turns in their youth. Another man quietly slipped his foot out from his prayer group's circle and, with it, took down one of the dancers following the singer. The dancer jumped in suspicious anger but could find no one to make eye contact with. Unsure as to what he'd tripped over, he was forced by the flow of his singing and dancing line to move on, filled with anger. A spirit of wickedness had seized much territory in this church.

That was it. Discord had shot fractures throughout the church, and it was ready to break apart. I'm not sure why I was so surprised by the situation. After all, this was exactly what I had written to them about in my letters. I had known that there was disunity and that those who prophesied were annoyed with those who spoke in tongues and such. I guess I just hadn't pictured what that would look like in physical terms. I never imagined there would be so many people; each group was large enough to function without *any* care for the others.

What in the world should I do now? Everyone participating in this debauchery needed to hear my letter read aloud, and they needed to follow it. But how to accomplish it? Then I remembered, we had already tried that, right?

"Timothy!" I said at once. "You've read them my letter, haven't you? The letter I sent with Sosthenes?"

Timothy's response was slightly indignant but also slightly guilty. "Yes, of course, I read it to them! But they refused to listen. I walked from end to end of the property, from group to group. 'Paul sends a letter!' 'I have a letter from Paul!' and almost everyone quieted down at first, eager to hear something new. But as soon as your words struck their immediate displeasure, they turned away and went back to their disruptive behavior. Each seems to think his method of praise is the proper one and, therefore, that everyone else should follow him and make him the church leader. Only a few listened to the letter until the end, and they generally seemed to accept your words as authoritative. But these more patient people had craved peace and order of worship long before your letter. Agreeing wholeheartedly with your words wasn't enough to empower them to change anything. Since I first landed here, many have drifted away from the livelier groups to the more peaceful, but there has been little significant overall change."

As Timothy was speaking, emotion left his voice and features, and he slipped into the demeanor of an outside observer, neutrally reporting the facts. As his speech came to a close, however, his tone and inflection picked up a bit as though champing at the bit for a command from me. He burned with desire to fix the situation and hoped I could give him the instructions. Stephenas, too, I trusted, would do anything that needed to be done, though the older man's eagerness didn't flare like Timothy's.

"What can I do? What can I do?" No, that wasn't right at all. I had let the chaotic situation clutter my thinking. "What will the Holy Spirit do through me?" There it was; that was the right question.

I turned to the others and told them that we had to pray for guidance from the Holy Spirit and for the Holy Spirit to bring peace to the Corinthian church. I felt humbled as I realized I was only using prayer as a fallback because of my own weakness when it should have been instinctual to start with prayer. I had no way to deal with this thorn in my flesh and could only rely on the Holy Spirit's power. I was, however, very impressed with young Timothy and Stephenas, who eagerly acknowledged the importance of submission to God for aid.

We had not been praying long, no more than an hour, when a man came running up, crying out, "Paul? It's Paul! Paul is here, everyone! Come listen to the great Paul!"

It appeared obvious that he had chosen to side with me against Apollos and Peter in the factional disputes. But after the man had whipped up a good deal of attention, his voice shifted to demeaning and jeering.

"Yes, that's right, Paul. It's Paul the apostle!" (He added extra sneer to the word "apostle.") "The apostle who was struck by the thunder and lightning of God—according to him." Then he jerked back into a tone of mock pleasantness. "The self-proclaimed apostle. Though there were already twelve apostles to match the twelve tribes of Israel, the Lord saw fit to appoint Paul as lucky apostle number thirteen. Not while He lived, as He had done for the original twelve, but in a magical apparition that only Paul himself can attest to. Paul the apostle? Ha! More like Simon Magus the Magician of Wickedness." He compared me with the first heretic, the man who thought he could buy the gospel. "More like Paul, Archenemy of the Great Peter!"

Timothy leaned over and whispered to me, "He's one of the leaders of the Peter faction."

"Thank you, Timothy," I replied. The silliness of his stating the obvious, however, broke up my rising embarrassment and anger, which otherwise could have hindered my judgment.

The situation looked dire, and there seemed to be only two options: start shouting my defense or turn and walk away. It's really no wonder that Timothy and Stephenas were unable to get any traction for reform in Corinth. But before I fell into despair, the squawking man ran out of clever things to say, and not knowing how to end his show, he handed the crowd over to me.

"So, Paul the Windbag, do you want to blow some hot air at us today?"

How could I make this work? With over half of the cars at my attention only listening for a chance to mock, would I do more harm than good by speaking? I had to neutralize the threat of being overtaken by a wave of cynical mockery. I had already concluded that this group was primarily made up of true Christians, even though they were in this pitiable state. These were my naughty children. They needed to be rebuked and to understand that they acted wrongly, but above all, they needed love. They needed to know that I loved them, that I was there for them, and that they could count on me, with the help of Christ, to take care of them.

The belligerent man had freely offered me an opportunity to speak, and time was ticking while I thought. First, loving affirmation for those who expect my opposition. Should I open with *I love you all*? No, too generic. It would have been blown off as empty rhetoric. I had to target the opposition. *Oh, of course!*

I thought. Those who "follow Peter" will be the more rigidly natured, more inclined to tradition and Jewish legalism. Those who "follow Paul" will be the more unconventional type. (This is ironic because I had been raised a legalist Pharisee.)

Rumors had spread far, fast, and wide about Peter and Paul's "big fight" in Antioch, where I had "blasted" Peter for acting like a Pharisee. That my ability to bring a situation to a head and Peter's humble strength in the face of public embarrassment fit perfectly for a resolution of complete unity had not traveled as fast. It would have been impossible to choose sides on strictly theological grounds, as Peter and I don't differ, but they had obviously done so on general perceptions of us and simply picked the caricature that best suited their own personalities.

This realization was quite funny to me. All the touchy-feelies of Corinth followed Paul, but Peter cried all the time; between the two of us, he was more the touchy-feely one by a long shot. His heartstrings were so accessible that he would break down with tears at the slightest emotional provocation. I'm not a stoic warrior, but I'm not nearly as emotionally inclined as Peter.

Finally, as the crowd's attention began to waver, I formed a rough plan. Rushing into step one I blurted out, "Honor to you, who, in honor of our Lord Jesus, eat only what is clean!" This startled everyone, even Timothy. "Honor to you, who study the ancient Scriptures, seeking the Truth of Jesus!" I was going to praise other groups I suspected of following Peter, but I could see the shock on their faces start to turn to distrust. So before distrust took them completely, and while I still had their attention, I turned to explanation. "You worship our Lord and Savior

Jesus Christ from the bottom of your hearts. You are filled with love for the one true God. This is plain to any who see you, and it overwhelms me with joy. I cannot help but feel overwhelming love for you." They seemed to grudgingly accept my love, knowing they would have to give up the nasty pleasure of hate they had so delighted in when thinking of me.

Step two. Back up to the broader community, and then make it clear I have authority here. "All you Corinthians! Look at the gifts the Holy Spirit has poured out to you! You are truly a blessed community. Your spontaneous song and dance for the Lord, your speaking in tongues, your prophets—all blessed with special gifts from the Holy Spirit for worshiping the Lord. I am truly honored to be an apostle to you, and my authority in the church at Corinth kindles the great love I have for you all."

Step three. Plant the seeds that will ultimately force the Corinthians to acknowledge that order is essential for their church. "But look at this situation. Each of you seems to use his gift to hinder the gifts of others! Can this truly be the will of Christ that during praise a singer interrupts a prophesier or that one in prayer trips a dancer?" Instantly, one face looked down and another wildly around, hoping to spot the accused. I probably shouldn't have used that example.

Step four. Refer them to the outline I had already given them for order in the church *(1 Corinthians)* and establish Stephenas as their go-to man for working out the details. "I've already explained in my letter how this is to be done. Stephenas holds the letter and can help you all to praise God each in your own way but in a civilized manner. Shall we read the letter to you now?"

Offering to read the letter may have been a mistake. "We've all… We've already read… heard it. It was read… I mean," stammered the belligerent man who had provided my introduction. The most vocal of those who spoke in tongues looked at me harshly, but when she opened her mouth, presumably to tell me off in a language I wouldn't have understood anyway, nothing came out.

Then, a hesitant voice squeaked, "Who cares if you love us? That doesn't make you right. You're still not the boss of us." And this little, almost-whimper encouraged another stronger voice to say, "We remember your letter, all right, Simon Magus! If I remember right, it said something like, 'Give me money! Give me money!'" Others joined him, taking up the cry that I was nothing but a fraud riding on Peter's coattails.

I looked around, and it was clear that the cry was not universal; only a few pushed it. But the majority of the crowd seemed to hide behind these mouthpieces as a defense against my embarrassing rebuke. They wanted to disappear, but hiding provides poor relief for stinging embarrassment.

The accusation itself left me floored. Even though as a teacher, helping them on their bridge to salvation, I would have been well within my right to demand payment, I never did so. I had worked my tail off to support myself primarily so that no one could make this claim, so that I could bring more people into the Way without them thinking I was in it for myself. My letter had asked them to set some money aside to help the poor Christians in Jerusalem, but it also spelled out that they could appoint honest men to accompany me and make sure every penny was faithfully delivered. Confusing this with me seeking personal gain was fully intentional. Did I blow it by asking them to help the Jerusalem church in my last letter? The Macedonians had given me some aid. Had I blown it by accepting? Or did I just blow it by coming here?

No, it was their duty to help their brothers in Jerusalem. I was right to ask for their aid. No, the Macedonians had helped me in my need, but not as much as I had helped them. I hadn't asked a penny for myself from the Corinthians, and the fact I had received aid from the Macedonians wasn't a valid excuse for them to reject the Truth. And no, I was right to have come here. I may have brought things to a head, and the Corinthian church very well might have collapsed under the arrogant strife of the Adversary at this point. But not coming, at best, would have only prolonged the fall of the church in Corinth and given the Adversary more time to revel in the chaos he had created.

I am embarrassed to admit that when these Corinthian rebels bombarded me with questions earthly emotions overtook me: indignation, embarrassment, rebuked love, sorrow, anger, and impotence. I lashed out, not exactly out of anger but as a man who arrives too late to put out a fire that engulfs his home. I flailed around, not knowing where to toss my tiny bucket of reason and knowing it would be useless.

What finally came out was this: "You know I supported myself when I was here! You know it! You know the money wasn't for me! You know I accept oversight for the money! How can you... You're avoiding the issue!" Then I felt a firm hand take my arm to pull me away and another gentler hand on my shoulder to comfort me.

"It's time to go," said Timothy with a solemn but unwavering voice.

I pulled myself together and announced clearly so that my stammering wouldn't be the last impression they had of me, "You have badly misused me, and worse, you've badly misused your gifts from the Holy Spirit."

With that, my two companions and I turned and quietly walked away. There was no jeering or laughing or other snide remarks when we left, just somber quiet as if at a funeral.

I often marveled at Timothy's ability to step up and correct me, his mentor. He was younger and less experienced but wise enough to provide the correction that I needed. He always seemed to look at me as if studying how he should behave. But when it was clear I needed some help, he didn't neglect his responsibility by saying that he was respecting his elder. Timothy is a remarkable young man. I think of him as a son and delight in him more than I can express.

A ship was to leave for Ephesus on the coming Tuesday, so we lingered at Stephenas's house the next day, steadily rebuilding the outward reflection of our ever-present inner joy. Stephenas expressed his intention to follow up on any progress I might have made. I was sure I had made none but kept the despairing thought to myself. I thanked Timothy for stepping up when he was needed, and no more was said about the subject.

The next day, we were on board a ship with the sea breeze providing us further refreshment. As we sailed, it struck me that we'd gone all the way to Corinth and hadn't even addressed the fact that some of the church was following a false gospel! My impulse was to return, but I knew my presence would only have made things worse. I was convinced that I'd dealt with the situation and rolled with the punches the best I could.

Had I tried to address the false gospel in person, I would have only stoked the fire of the behavior I had seen. But the gospel! There is only one gospel, and those who don't stand on it are condemned to death eternal. Maybe I should have hit hard with my message of one gospel and driven that division deeper, splitting the church. Those of the one true gospel, then, could grow afresh with the weeds removed. But the Corinthian church had boomed so fast and in such an unorganized manner that perhaps many who gave ear to the forked tongues of the false gospels had only halfheartedly listened and hadn't committed to the heresy.

Also, bringing it up during the confrontation may have legitimatized the false doctrine as an up-for-discussion theological issue. Focusing on getting them to just look at themselves and their behavior was assuredly the best policy. If they could control their behavior and temper their arrogance, the Truth would be plain. And then, the wayward with honest hearts would turn to the real gospel.

But it continued to weigh on my heart. They must have the one true gospel, with no others. The boat ride back to Ephesus gave me too much time to question myself.

Back at Ephesus

Still on the ship to Ephesus, I decided, "One more time. One more chance. I'll send one more letter." And I knew that this letter was going to hurt to write. It was going to cut to the heart of everything and lay the matter out for the Corinthians in no uncertain terms. It would be a fire-and-brimstone letter demanding the Corinthians adhere to the one true gospel. It would be a tearful letter for me to write. And when I settled in at Ephesus and began to dictate to Sosthenes, I had to pause several times to collect myself back from tears. *(This was the third letter of four that we know Paul wrote to the Corinthians; it is now lost. Paul would write 2 Corinthians, which is included in the Bible, at a later date.)*

I started by recapping the painful visit Timothy and I had just made to them. I used the recap to lay out the exact problems they were having. Then I harshly rebuked them and warned that they couldn't chase off God's judgment as easily as they had convinced me to leave in my humility. They knew that I preached the true gospel and that I had true authority as an apostle. Chasing me off and denying any authority contrary to their will equated to attempting to hide from God. I tremble remembering my fear for the Corinthians, who were more like children to me because of the amount of help they needed from me.

Unfortunately, this letter was far from perfect as I hadn't really given myself enough time to think everything through and develop a plan. I wrote the letter with my instinct-to-action still driving. In short, I told the Corinthians I was going to come straight back soon and wanted them to have their act together before I got there. Of course, once my reason replaced emotion, I realized that they might profit from more time without me. I changed my mind. I went north through Macedonia instead of following what I said in my earlier letter. This change of plans gave my enemies in Corinth a sliver of truth to promote their lie that I constantly waffle. (And this from people who are constantly comparing me to Peter!)

Timothy volunteered to carry this letter, but I good-naturedly laughed at his offer. The Corinthians had beaten him down as harshly as they had me, and he apparently wanted more misuse. We both needed a break from the Corinthians. It was time for him to refresh himself in other matters that were sure to have more positive experiences mixed in. I thought a fresh-faced deliverer would better prepare the Corinthians to receive the contents of my newest letter.

I gave the letter to Titus to carry. He wasn't a lot older than Timothy, and both became like sons to me, though, if compelled, I would have to admit that Timothy always held the most central place in my heart. Timothy would have burst with enthusiasm and energy if very sound judgment hadn't so properly restrained him. Titus didn't lack in any of these qualities, and he always gave me the impression that he followed Timothy as his example even though Timothy was the younger.

So it was decided that Titus would take the letter to Corinth and stay there as long as he and Stephenas thought it useful. If the Holy Spirit were to call him to move, he was to send word to us as soon as possible. Likewise, we would let him know if we were to depart Ephesus. Off he went for that challenging city.

My first months in Ephesus had been the most dramatic with the seven sons of Sceva and the whole Corinthian mess, but I was there for three full years. And each of those years saw huge numbers of souls turning to Christ. (I wasn't exactly in Ephesus the entire time; Ephesus was more like a home base. I resided with Aquila and Priscilla but took countless trips throughout Turkey in that period, usually for less than two weeks each time.) Timothy remained at my side, watching and learning from me, but more importantly, practicing. Timothy had always preached boldly, and he was ever increasing in skill and growing in the Word.

At this point, we couldn't help but feel positive about our work for the Lord in Ephesus and all of Turkey. We had been there for three years, made measurable headway for the Lord, and personally supported the developing communities as their roots grew strong. Large numbers had turned to the Lord and actively worked to grow deeper in His Word. The number of Christian leaders in western Turkey proliferated so that each local church was led by a strong captain. Everything worked together so that these local churches could develop into a system of mutual support for individuals, making the path of establishing themselves in Christ as smooth as possible.

The news from Corinth also provided encouragement. But Titus had been delinquent in sitting down and preparing a full, detailed account of the situation for me. I wasn't sure exactly how reliable the secondhand accounts were, and the few letters I received from Titus were scant. He had obviously dashed them off in a rush, usually ending in promises to write more later. It always amazed me how Titus, who possessed such unfailing energy in so many matters, seemed so utterly devoid of the ability to sit his butt down and write a simple but full letter. So, while the news I had from Corinth pleased me, I took care to restrain my expectations.

To be completely honest, once I made it back to Ephesus from that disastrous Corinthian visit, I didn't spend a great deal of time thinking about Corinth. I trusted Titus. He would have returned if Corinth had truly been a lost cause, and he would have called for me if he thought I could help. His letters had been hastily written and short but overall positive. What a fool I'd be to rock that boat if Titus's efforts were slowly starting to pay off! Besides, Timothy and I weren't twiddling our thumbs. We prayed with great hope for Corinth. The rest of the time, we were simply too busy in Turkey for our thoughts to roam to Greece.

By the end of our third year in Ephesus, I was convinced that the local churches of Turkey were firmly established under trustworthy and competent leaders. The melancholy side of this coin was that I couldn't help feeling that I was no longer useful. I can't say I lacked the temptation to stay in Ephesus and bask in the joy that Jesus had brought, but I knew my work there was done. The Lord hadn't commissioned me to bask.

Timothy and I began to work out our departure plan. We would go through Macedonia and Greece before returning to Syrian Antioch, but we weren't sure of our route. Corinth presented the difficulty. On one hand, it was *the* place I most longed to visit. On the other, I still feared my presence might upset Titus's work.

I wanted my visit to be joyful, but did they need a little more time to reach full repentance?

We spent entirely too long discussing this, but we ultimately decided to head into Macedonia and then work our way down through Greece. We would have Titus meet us in Troas or somewhere along the way if possible. If not, we would see him in Corinth. From there, we would determine the particulars of our return to Syrian Antioch and Jerusalem. Aquila fired off a quick letter letting Titus know that we would leave Ephesus in about two weeks and that we hoped he could meet us on the way.

I was probably overeager to get the ball rolling now that the decision was made. So, the next day, I sent Timothy and our brother Erastus ahead to Macedonia to start softening the ground for strong roots. Leaving Ephesus would prove to personally benefit Timothy and Erastus more than any of us had expected. As it turned out, the Ephesians had saved us one more dramatic episode.

Demetrius and the Craftsmen

An incident erupted as I prepared to depart Ephesus. A craftsman named Demetrius starkly reminded us that opposition to the Way was still formidable. Demetrius was a silversmith who had become increasingly agitated by dwelling on his concern for dropping sales. He made little shrines to Artemis, one of the Greek gods, and other temple trinkets. The way he saw it, which, of course, was accurate, the more people who turned to Jesus, the fewer people there were to buy his junk.

Demetrius wasn't the only craftsman who was upset. They all came together, and Demetrius addressed them: "Paul is turning people away from our gods and our products! He claims that the works of our own hands aren't gods at all. This is where your money comes from, and he's persuading people throughout all of Turkey not to buy your gods and goods! He's trying to make a joke of your entire profession. As of now, all of Turkey, and even the entire world, worships the great goddess Artemis. But if Paul has his way, she will be overthrown by his Jesus; she will count for nothing!"

Demetrius's linking their financial well-being to the supposed greatness of Artemis got the attention of his audience. Amazing how often people mix their financial well-being with piety, isn't it?

The craftsmen's anger erupted, pushing the city to the edge of riot. In their excited state, the craftsmen could think of nothing more than to simply yell out, "Great is Artemis of the Ephesians!" over and over again. They snatched up two of my traveling companions and dragged them to the theater, where public events and debate were held. The whole city was worked up into a confused storm by this time. When one man saw another go to the theater, he went too, without understanding the purpose. Some people cried out completely unrelated grievances, and initially only a few people had any idea why they were there at all. But everyone knew something exciting was happening.

My inclination was to get involved, to get right up there in the thick of it to support my brothers in Christ. Other disciples, though, blocked my desire. My friends pressed me hard to keep my head down and mouth shut. Initially, physical restraint was necessary. Different voices, firm but from friends, yelled at me, "You can't help!" "Do you really think *you* can make this situation *better*?" "What do you think is going to happen if you go marching up there? The mob will snap and kill you all with no benefit to the Kingdom! Do you want your friends to die? Then don't go!" Slowly, their pleas sank in, and I took their counsel, remaining in the background as a spectator with a heavy heart.

By this time, enough of the mob had gotten the gist of the situation: those brought before them were challenging Artemis and her authority. They were also aware that the town clerk himself was a Jew, a worshiper of a foreign god, who rejected the greatness of their pretty Artemis. They ignored him as he motioned for silence. So the intermittent yells of "Great is Artemis of the Ephesians!" turned into a chant, and they yelled it for two hours, rivaling even the most monotonous of church services.

Finally, the town clerk quieted the crowd, though I expect it was less his doing and more that the crowd just wore themselves out with all the chanting. The clerk's speech was sharp, to the point, and brief: "Everyone knows that Ephesus is where the sacred stone fell out of the sky."

Even amid such heavy danger, this mythical nonsense made me snicker. The town clerk went on, "Ephesus is home to the temple of the great Artemis! Why are you acting so rashly when no one can deny it? Settle down! You dragged these men here, men who have not blasphemed our goddess; they only prefer a different god. But the courts are available! Demetrius and his craftsmen can take them there, to the courts, if they have a real grievance. This is a civilized town; take your trouble to the courts if you have a legitimate complaint! There is no reason for all this uproar. Your nonsensical behavior puts us in real danger of being charged by the Romans with rioting." He was afraid of a harsh Roman reaction to the ridiculous outburst of the Ephesian people. The Romans like order, and the town clerk knew that they would restore it if he couldn't.

With this, the clerk dismissed the assembly, and to the relief of anyone with common sense, they dispersed. The town clerk's statements were all obviously true. We were not directly blaspheming Artemis. The courts were available to handle grievances. The city was out of control. The Romans were likely to draw swords. Not to mention the rabble had exhausted themselves with all of their silly chanting.

Still, I can't say there was no truth in Demetrius's statements. We were actively bringing people to Christ, which meant we were taking them away from Artemis and the craftsmen's trinkets. All in all, though, the situation could have turned out much worse, and if I'd pushed myself forward when it was hottest, it probably would have.

So the great ruckus in Ephesus had erupted and fizzled out, and the Christians had escaped with no more than a bit of rough handling, although it was quite rough handling. The interruption having proven temporary, my plans to leave town weren't only back on, but bumped up. Yes, everything had settled down, but experience had taught me that the threatening animosity wouldn't be so easily tamed. Major, unsatisfied hostility boiled beneath the surface, ever ready for violent outburst.

The church in Turkey could survive without me. And since I seemed to be the flashpoint for most of the violence, it might even survive better without me for a while. To "tie up loose ends" only meant cushioning my departure with friendly visits. Now, it seemed more prudent to skip all that and get out of town. I left the next day.

Smyrna, Pergamum, and Troas

A hasty departure sent me north around the sea on my way to Corinth. I traveled up the west coast of Asia through Smyrna and Pergamum on my way to Troas. Here, I hoped to find Titus on his way back to Ephesus from Corinth, even though I had left Ephesus sooner than expected.

Of course, I'd been to both Smyrna and Pergamum on short visits from Ephesus over the past several years. The local churches had been established, and my purpose for stopping was to better establish them in the Word. Looking back, I probably spent too much time in Smyrna and not enough in Pergamum, but managing my time wasn't usually something I had to think about. I'd go somewhere and work until I was comfortable moving on or until pushed by the Spirit to move on.

One benefit of having been forced from Ephesus was that we caught up with Timothy and Erastus as soon as we got to Smyrna. They'd only had a day's head start before Demetrius gave me my cue to leave. Because they'd expected us to tail by at least a week, they were shocked to see us. They were also somewhat surprised to learn that such a major eruption of anger had occurred when everything had seemed fairly smooth. Timothy looked disappointed to have missed it, and I was a little jealous of him because my youthful eagerness for such situations to prove myself had waned considerably.

The people of Smyrna were poor, but they were strong in their faith. I delighted in teaching them as they were not only eager to learn but also to do their best to live solid Christian lives. And they were not weak-willed and ready to follow any teacher of new things. Once instructed in the true gospel, they were ever on their guard against false teachings.

Pergamum, on the other hand, gave us a harder time. Generally, I have to say that the people of Pergamum held fast to the true faith. But they provided too safe a harbor for false teachers and distorters of the Way, even for the vilest of them. They also suffered difficulty breaking from their earthly habits, rushing to sexual immorality and ceremonial feasts of food sacrificed to idols. Still, they were open to teaching, so I hold out hope for them. But I probably left Pergamum too soon.

In the end, what was my reward for abandoning Pergamum when I could have spent more time feeding her roots? Heartbreak and disappointment in Troas. My eagerness to see Titus had drawn me from Pergamum, but he wasn't in Troas when I arrived. I thought I'd given him plenty of time to get to Troas before me, and I fully expected to see him there. But then again, he wouldn't have known of our early departure from Ephesus.

Disappointed but not letting that funk overtake me, I set about working for the Lord. Church establishment in Troas went as such: plant, water, weed, feed, grow. I'd previously planted this local church, so now it was time to further establish it in the Word, strengthening its roots so they could support a strong, flowering church. And while I focused on strengthening the existing congregation, the church also burst with new members. I hadn't expected it, but the doors to the hearts of many in Troas opened to me.

During my visit to Troas, I took a short trip to the neighboring town of Assos, where I also had great success, much to my joy. I'd intended to stop in Assos on my way to Troas. The success we had bringing people into the Way in Troas and Assos refreshed me with the reminder that His grace is sufficient regardless of my personal shortcomings, especially when it comes to planning.

I lingered in Troas many days beyond what I expected, but that was what the situation required as the flood to Christ continued. Besides, I hadn't promised anyone I would keep a strict schedule. I will admit that I welcomed the extra time in Troas. I had an unreasonable expectation that Titus would show up at any minute. He never did, but the work we completed for Christ there was a great condolence.

Eventually, the time came to move on to Macedonia. Troas was a port city in the far northwest of Turkey, so the ride to the Macedonian port city of Neapolis was short and sweet. Still, something about sitting on a boat always made me eager for action. I cycled through scenarios of what I would do and say in Macedonia, energizing myself ahead of my task to spread the Word. We weren't off the boat for five minutes before I started preaching in Neapolis. Within twenty minutes of our landing, conflict pressed us. And within an hour, I was in jail.

Neapolis

Darn it! I'd grown accustomed to success for the Lord in Turkey, and now I was in a Macedonian prison in Neapolis. If I'm completely honest, part of me was happy to be locked up, safe from the rabble of pagan belligerents. Danger of physical injury seemed to spike as soon as we landed in Macedonia, and with it, our fear.

We certainly had faced opposition, even beatings, in Turkey. After all, it was only a few months since Demetrius and the craftsmen had attacked us in Ephesus. But over time, familiarity dampened our opposition. Most Turkish nonbelievers had stopped seeing us as a threat to their established customs and had become comfortable simply making fun of us. Our threat to the craftsmen's pocketbooks was the exception, not the norm.

A few of us were arrested on occasion as we pressed the Word to more and more people, and we were roughed up from time to time too. But the outbreaks of real, life-threatening danger had pretty much subsided early in our Turkish stay.

Everything changed as soon as we set foot in Macedonia. That real, life-threatening danger flared, and I expected it to follow us through Macedonia, maybe even farther. This was the first time I felt tired and weary. I didn't want to get beat up anymore. My years of experience started to feel like a weight on my shoulders, and for the first time in my life, I couldn't defeat the apprehension I felt about potential beatings by forcing myself to boldness.

The jailer came to our room shortly after our arrest. He was neither friendly nor antagonistic; he was one of those seen-it-all
types. "Look. We really don't want to deal with this. We don't
care about you or your Jesus or the stupid people who bobble
around after you. But we're not putting up with the problems
you cause either. Everything has settled down enough, but it'll
all blow up again if we let you out now. You can go tomorrow
if you *go*. Got it?" His emphasis on the word "go" made it clear
that we were to leave the city.

Oh, well. Neapolis is Philippi's port city; they're not a day's walk
apart. The leaders of the local church in Philippi still had a long
way to go before they were firmly established, but on the job
is the best way to learn (undeniably when it's the only option).
They could start to commune with Neapolis, and the two cities
could grow together. Not that it really mattered for my planning;
there was nothing more I could do in Neapolis. If I were to try,
it was clear I would either be arrested, or, which was more likely,
the city magistrates would simply look the other way while our
antagonists killed me. The next day, I was quietly off to Philippi.

To Philippi

The walk through the district of Philippi was quiet, and as my
eyes wandered over the land, I thought about how many generations had walked over it as they passed in and out of time. I
must have been already getting old, dwelling on the greatness
of the land itself and reminiscing on things in which I had no
part. To help further ease the Macedonian fear that had taken
root in Neapolis, Luke and I conversed in more-solemn-than-
need-be tones about the Roman colony Philippi and its past.

As we neared the city, the place where that wonderful lady, Lydia, embraced the Christ came into view, and our conversation turned to our own exploits in Philippi: the possessed slave girl whom I freed, our imprisonment, the jailer whose name I've forgotten, his conversion, and the joy of Lydia. This was the first place Luke had been with us after he left his home in Troas, so it seemed fitting that he was my traveling companion now. I confessed to him that I hadn't expected him to stick around after the wild ride Philippi had given us on our earlier visit.

Luke found my confession greatly amusing. As he reflected on our last visit to the city, he explained, "I was seriously thinking about leaving before Philippi. Everything was sketchy in my head, and from the second we left Troas, I felt like an idiot for going with you. It was in Philippi that my faith was firmly established. From Troas, I'd been on board intellectually, but it wasn't until you were singing in the Philippian prison, and I was overcome with that deep-seated joy, that I truly turned myself over to Jesus. I was a bit scared with you and Silas in prison, but that earthquake and the jailer's turning to the Lord—wow! It was as if God had done it all just to let me know how real Christ is. I'm not so arrogant to think it really was all for me, but that's how it felt.

"I realized that up until that point, I'd only been pulled along by some curious philosophical interest. By the time we left Philippi, the joy and love of Christ had completely beaten any fear or doubt out of me. I was still interested intellectually, of course, but God had so embedded His Truth in my heart that I just knew it better than any formulaic proof could ever teach me.

So the idea that I might have left at the very point that my heart committed is hysterical!"

As we were talking, we naturally paused when we came to the place where Lydia had been baptized. Now we stood looking nostalgically at the water.

"I wonder," I started. "I wonder what people will remember of our effort." Then it struck me that my words might not sound quite right; I may have sounded too self-important. So, I continued, fumbling a bit in my embarrassment, "I'm just curious. I mean, I imagine that even I've already forgotten much of what I've done. I suppose that it isn't important *how*, so long as the Church endures."

"No. It is important," Luke said calmly. "Do you think that the gospel will cover the entire earth to every inhabited region before you die? I'm not much younger than you, so I'll be out of the picture not long after you. Timothy and Titus follow your methods closely, and many may learn from them, but they are only two. Peter and the others, I'm sure, are doing a great job and probably all have people learning under them. But let's face it: their methods aren't nearly as effective and efficient as yours at scale. Knowing how the Church grew after Jesus could be important."

When I caught myself enjoying what he was saying a bit more than I ought to have, I checked my pride and interrupted him jokingly, "Are you forming the new Paul faction?"

Luke laughed but didn't reply in jest. "I do follow Paul. And I follow Peter. And I follow James, and on and on," he said. "You're the apostles specially commissioned by God. And who am I?"

"You're our great physician. With so much violence pointed at us, the Christians may need you more than they need me!"

"Or, at least, they need me *because* of you." Luke was joking, and I was the one who had pushed the conversation to lightheartedness. But his quip struck a sour note to my ears because I had often wondered if I was doing more harm than good.

"Hey," Luke interrupted my thoughts. "You pray, and you're open to the Spirit. And just look at what the Spirit has done through you. Less than half the local churches would exist if it weren't for you, and there would probably be four times as many false gospels." He paused as if distracted by another thought. "More Christians need to follow your model: plant a church, then strengthen it, plant a church, then strengthen it…"

"It was funny, you know?"

"Huh? What was funny?" Luke came back from his thoughts.

"That we need your physician skills because of me. It was funny."

"Oh, yeah. I know it was. That's why I didn't apologize." Luke smiled broadly, and we walked on happily but without speaking anymore.

We were close to Philippi's gates when several brothers came out to greet us. "Titus!" I yelled when I realized it was him.

Philippi

Titus, of course, had expected me to leave Ephesus more than a week after my forced early departure. He had decided to pass through the churches in Greece and Macedonia and hoped to run into me in a week or so in Troas. Now he was bursting to tell us how his trip was going. Doors had opened for him to preach the Word in every hut and hovel throughout Macedonia. I was thrilled, of course, but having just been booted out of Neapolis perhaps also a little jealous.

But this wasn't all that fueled Titus's state of explosive joy. He had great news from Corinth. I'd been anxious for Titus and Corinth since Troas. Now here we were, and he unloaded all the great news. The overwhelming majority of the Corinthians were truly repentant for their behavior; they set their vices aside and prayed to God for forgiveness. There was even one believer guilty of particularly crude and immoral behavior whom the church ostracized in accordance with my previous letter. This individual was now fully repentant and wanted nothing more than to be allowed back into communion with the community.

We sat down that very day to fire off another letter to the church in Corinth. *(This letter would become 2 Corinthians of the Bible. It is the fourth and final letter that we know Paul wrote to the Corinthians.)*

Our energy came from our eagerness to express to Corinth the joy we had for them, but there were other important points to hit too.

For one, they needed to let that repentant sinner back into the community. The main purpose to shame with ostracism is to help pull the ostracized member back into the community. Once truly repentant, he ought not to be left alone in such grief.

I also wanted the church to be prepared for my coming. They had promised to get a collection together for the poor in Jerusalem, and I didn't want them to be embarrassed by not having it when I got there. And on top of this, I really couldn't help telling them how thrilled I was to send Titus to them, as he and I were of the same heart.

While the news was overwhelmingly positive, not all the problems had been wiped out. A small and dwindling minority still rebelled against my letters and held to false apostles among them. I'd been too overjoyed with the general news of Corinth, so the thought of these false apostles didn't really bother me until we sat down to write the letter. When we did, I found myself getting riled up and even sarcastic. The few who still clung to these deceivers seemed to regard them as super-apostles, closer to the angels than to man.

By this point, my work for the Lord had landed me in prison repeatedly, I'd suffered beatings beyond count, five times I'd been whipped with thirty-nine lashes, and three times I'd been beaten with rods. I'd been shipwrecked three times (not counting a future shipwreck I would live through as a prisoner on my way to Rome). I'd even been stoned, for crying out loud. Why in the world did these few Corinthians cling to these "super-apostles"? Did they show more dedication than I?

But since the news was mostly positive, so, too, was my letter. Titus was up at the crack of dawn, rushing back to Corinth to give the Corinthians a reasonable amount of time to react to this letter before my arrival.

The rest of us spent several days strengthening the church in Philippi before continuing. Theoretically, it was the perfect setup. Titus had rushed back to Corinth, and we would continue stopping and strengthening the churches on our way to meet him there, which would work out just right for timing. Practically, we were so eager to be in Corinth that some of us did have trouble staying focused as we passed through Macedonia and Greece.

Finally, we were in Corinth.

Third and Final Corinthian Visit

When we arrived in Corinth, the believer Gaius came out of his house to greet us before we even made it to his door. He had been watching for our coming for days. "They repent! We repent!" were the first words out of his mouth, and with them, he blasted away our traveler's fatigue. We all entered his house in high spirits.

When Gaius had first spoken, we remembered the news from the letter and felt joy. But Gaius's statement had had more than one meaning. Evidently, my last letter had destroyed the confidence of those holding out in rebellion. After the letter was read out loud, all but one or two of the Corinthians abandoned the super-apostles. At first, they just slunk away as if they had never been part of that circle, but when some of the stronger members of the congregation pressed them, they openly renounced the super-apostles and their teachings. Deprived of followers and confronted with the fact that I would soon be there, the super-apostles disappeared.

We remained in Corinth over the winter, but this initial meeting set the tone for the rest of our stay, a truly joyful three months. The joyous atmosphere, however, only amplified my restlessness for action.

I had wanted to go to Rome for some time. My general plan was to use Rome as a home base from which to launch the gospel into Spain. The churches I had planted on the eastern side of the Roman Empire flourished, and the proverbial untouched fields ripe for harvest in Spain on the western side of the empire captivated me. It would be just like old times. I decided that after I took the collection to Jerusalem, I would execute this plan, so I wrote a letter to the church in Rome in part to explain my intent. *(This is the book of Romans of the New Testament.)*

I had taken up a significant collection throughout Greece, Macedonia, and Turkey for the needy brothers and sisters in Jerusalem. It amazed me that people as poor as the Macedonians would give so much to help others, and now the Corinthians also came through as they said they would.

As I prepared to leave Corinth for my return to Jerusalem, I learned that the Jews here, too, plotted against me. *Et tu,* Corinth? In fact, the situation provided me very little trouble. For one, I had already planned on departing. For two, I was almost pleased at trouble coming from *outside* the Corinthian church for a change. I felt Corinth could now stand up to anything the outside world could throw at them.

I had representatives with me from all the different areas I had taken collections from. They weren't only to keep me honest; they were also tasked with keeping me and the collection safe from robbers. Thus, we were a large party when we left Corinth, heading back north over land through Greece and into Macedonia.

When we got to Philippi, I sent some of our party ahead to Troas. The rest of us settled into Philippi for the Days of Unleavened Bread. After the festival, we sailed to Troas to reorganize in the western Turkish town on our way back to Jerusalem.

Back in Troas

We stayed in Troas in western Turkey for a week, and the night before departing was quiet and slow. The disciples gathered to break bread in a stuffy, third-story room. There were plenty of lamps, so I was able to speak on about the Lord late into the calm night. I did so until about midnight when Eutychus, whose name means "lucky," fell asleep.

Eutychus was a young man of fleeting attention. Struggling to stay awake and keep up with the conversation, he had propped himself up against the window, hoping the cool air would aid his efforts. He failed. He fell into sleep and out of the window.

His body dropped the three stories to the ground where its accelerating motion ended with an abrupt thud. Then his body didn't move at all. When I made it down to him the slow way, someone had already picked up his lifeless body, which I then took into my arms. As I held the young man, his life quietly returned to him. I greatly comforted the disciples, telling them that they shouldn't be alarmed and that Eutychus held his life. I handed the young man off for care and returned to the upper floor to break bread, eat, and continue in conversation under a sense of quiet peace until daybreak. And at daybreak, I departed.

The local disciples returned to their homes, carrying the lucky young man with them. The other disciples, my traveling companions, I sent by ship to a bigger port city. I would meet them there after traveling by land to wrap up a few things. I especially wanted to stop in at several places on the way to encourage those who had previously turned to Christ.

Message to the Elders of Ephesus at Miletus

After my short journey by land, I boarded the little coast-cruising boat with the others and sailed off. I was eager to make it to Jerusalem. I wanted to be there before the Feast of Pentecost began, if possible. We sailed past Ephesus without stopping, even though I needed to speak with the local church elders there. So when we landed in Miletus, I sent a message to the Ephesian church elders, calling them to come to me. (This was all still on the western coast of Turkey, and Ephesus is only about ten miles or so from Miletus, so it wasn't such a major request.) I was convinced this would be the last chance I had to talk to them, and I wasn't going to miss my opportunity. When the church elders began to show up from Ephesus, we chatted casually until they all arrived.

"Hey, I heard about that kid who jumped out the window to get away from your speech," said one of the first elders to arrive.

Then, "I guess people are jumping out of windows now to get away from your talks," jested a latter arrival. Teasing me about Eutychus's fall was going to be a thing.

Once everyone arrived, I addressed the group. "You know how I lived the entire time I was with you. I served the Lord with humility, tears, and trials. I suffered plot after plot from the Jews. I taught in public, and I taught from house to house. I taught everything worth teaching you without shrinking from controversial topics. I testified to Jews. I testified to Gentiles. I preached repentance toward God, and I taught faith in Jesus Christ." Not to sound self-important, but truly, this is how I had lived. And people needed an example to follow. These people had my life as an example, and I wanted to encourage them to follow it.

Why was I telling them this now? Well, that's what I explained next. "The Spirit compels me to go to Jerusalem. I'm not exactly sure how it will play out, but everywhere I've been, the Holy Spirit has made it clear to me that I shouldn't expect a good time. I don't know the specifics, but imprisonment and afflictions await me in that city. I can handle those. In fact, so long as I can finish the course of my ministry, which the Lord Jesus has commissioned me, my physical well-being and even my life are of little value to me. Let it be, so long as I can finish my mission of preaching the gospel and the grace of our Lord and Savior Jesus Christ! In fact, I know none of you will see my face again." That's why it had been so important to converse with them.

And, having saved the major point for last, I laid it out. "I've told you everything I could so that you may find salvation in Jesus Christ. If you blow it now, it's on your own heads. But more importantly, you are the overseers of the church. The Holy Spirit placed you in this position. Pay close attention to yourselves and to the flock you are responsible for. Sometime after I leave, fierce wolves will come in among you and tear the sheep to shreds. And even from yourselves will come twisted speech from twisted tongues to lead disciples away from the Truth and down twisted paths. Be on guard against them, and save as much of the flock as you can." This was the most important point, but I feared it may not have had enough impact. Many seemed to be too distracted by anguish to be fully attentive after I had told them they would not see me again.

(As I had warned, it later came true. The church at Ephesus has been pillaged by false teachers, some of whom had been among the elders of the local church. By their permissiveness, they manipulated people to follow them away from Christ. Their substance-free preaching provided them with an easily-built following, and they wallowed in the conceit that their superficial following provided them.)

I capped off my little sermon by again advising them to follow me as an example of how they should act. I commended them to God before reminding them that I hadn't coveted the silver, gold, or clothing of others and that I had always worked with my own hands to meet my own needs as well as the needs of others. I was undeniably doing God's work spreading the Gospel, but I didn't demand that others pay my way to ease my exertions. I had been on display for them, showing that we are to work hard to help the weak. As Jesus had told his followers, it is more blessed to give than it is to receive.

There was a lot of weeping at my departure. The disciples found it particularly distressing that they would not see me again. We knelt on the ground, and I prayed with all of them. I embraced and kissed them, and they me. Then, they accompanied me to my ship, expecting to never see me again.

A Phoenician Town

We made many stops on the way back to Jerusalem, and I was able to stay with disciples along the route. We eventually had to board a sturdier ship, one more capable of open-sea travel than the little coast-hugger we had been traveling on. After the long voyage, about four hundred miles, we landed in Tyre in Phoenicia, where the ship's captain needed to unload his cargo.

We stayed with the disciples here for seven days. They constantly told me—according to them, "through the Spirit" —not to go to Jerusalem. I assumed that the Spirit had simply been warning them of the dangers I would face in Jerusalem and that they misinterpreted this to mean I shouldn't go. I know for a fact that the Spirit was telling me to go.

Being a Jew myself, I knew the ancient story about "the Man of God from Judah," from the time when Judah was ruled by kings. God told the man, whose name is lost to us, to go to Bethel to pronounce condemnation on all the altars and the trinket-worship that King Jeroboam was supporting. The Lord had also told the man of God not to eat or drink within a certain geographical area that he had to pass through to perform his task. But a prophet who lived in this area met him along the way and told him—one prophet to another—that an angel had told him that they were to eat together in the prophet's house, which was in this no-food zone. The man of God, setting aside his direct instructions, assumed that the message from the angel must have meant that God had changed his mind, so he ate. The prophet, however, had lied.

The consequence was that the Lord sent a lion to destroy the man of God for his transgression. So the moral of the story is this: If God says do it, you do it unless He directly tells you not to. If someone else has apparently contradictory information, it is not to be considered release from responsibility *(1 Kings 13)*.

I didn't expect that the other disciples were lying to me as the prophet from the story had, but I knew what I was told to do, and I knew they hadn't the authority to change my commission. The Spirit was plainly telling me to continue, so I continued. The local disciples accompanied me to the beach, where we knelt and prayed before saying our goodbyes. I boarded the ship with my traveling companions, and the local believers returned to their homes.

Caesarea: Philip's House

Finally, after only one more stop, we landed in Caesarea, Jerusalem's nearest major port city. In Caesarea, we stayed for many days at Philip the evangelist's house. He had four unmarried daughters, and all of them had been given the gift of prophecy.

While we were there, another prophet came from Judea to visit Philip's house-of-prophets. This was Agabus, the man who had prophesied the coming Jerusalem famine so that we were able to better prepare our less fortunate brothers.

Not long after Agabus arrived at Philip's house, he took my belt from me. Prophets were known to be theatrical, and Agabus, whom we all knew well, was no exception. So, when he took my belt, the situation wasn't as awkward as it may sound; we knew something interesting was coming.

He used the belt to bind his own hands and feet and announced, "In Jerusalem, the Jews will bind this belt's owner just like this!"

The disciples with me at Philip's house remembered their Christian brothers who had tried to dissuade me from continuing my undertaking, and this dramatic display pushed their nerves over the edge. They wept; some even sobbed without restraint and begged me not to push on to Jerusalem.

But I knew my mission. Agabus's demonstration was more poetically conveyed, and he was a well-known prophet, but ultimately, he had no more authority to cancel my orders than any of the others. Agabus, however, never once suggested I not go to Jerusalem. He only said I should expect to be bound once there. The Holy Spirit commanded me to go to Jerusalem, and unless He told me otherwise, I was determined to go. So, growing somewhat tired of the emotional pleas, I admonished the disciples: "Why are you carrying on crying and crying, begging me not to go? I am going, and all you are doing is breaking my heart. I am ready to suffer prison or even death for the name of the Lord Jesus." At this, they agreed to let the will of the Lord be done and put more effort into sucking it up.

CHAPTER 4:

Conflict and Bureaucracy

Jerusalem

(Now, around AD 57, Paul returns to Jerusalem. The narrative in Acts continues, but Paul has finished his third and final missionary journey recorded in that book.)

So my traveling companions and I put the sixty-two-mile journey from Caesarea to Jerusalem behind us, and arrived in the city on a beautiful spring day.

Some of the disciples from Caesarea accompanied us, and they knew a Jerusalem man who had been a long-time believer. They led us to his house, and we lodged there.

The brothers in Jerusalem were happy to receive us, and we were happy to be there. The day after we arrived, we went down to meet with James, the brother of the Lord, and all the elders of the local church in Jerusalem.

Speaking a little louder than normal, James said, "Hey, I heard about that kid who fell from the window in Troas."

The he-jumped-to-get-away-from-your-speech joke had been getting a bit old, at least for me, so I thought I would cut him off and beat him to the punch. "Yes, I know. He didn't fall—he jumped," I said with caricature-like exasperation.

"Oh, no!" replied James very seriously. "I was just going to mention that it's appropriate his name means Lucky. He really was lucky." Then James smiled slightly and added, "Lucky he had the window to escape from your speech." Oh, wonderful, a new variation on the joke. Clearly, this was going to be a thing.

When James and the elders heard the narrative of all the things God had done among the Gentiles through my ministry, they glorified and praised God. But then, the mood sobered as they warned us about the Jerusalem Jews' cold sentiment toward me. Overwhelmingly, word in town was that I had been running around through Gentile lands, teaching the Jews to forsake Moses, circumcision, tradition, and basically all things Jewish.

Of course, this was all untrue, but the perception was strong. Regardless of the truth, these Jews would eventually learn that I was in town and freak out. The danger to me, and the other disciples because of my presence, was significant.

To help alter the perception that I was anti-Jewish or anti-custom, James and the elders devised a plan. They advised me to take four young men who were under a Nazarite vow, purify myself at the temple with them, and even pay their way. This would display to the world that I lived according to the law and that the rumors they indulged in simply could not be true.

So I took the four young men with me, went to the temple, and began the seven-day purification process. The young men had already been purified when they began their vow, but I gave notice at the temple that when my purification was complete, I would present the offering for myself and for each of the four young men.

Jerusalem Conflict

Unfortunately, near the end of my seven-day purification, some Jews from Turkey took notice of me. I was there to help my image in front of the Jerusalem Jews, and I expected that I could reason with them when noticed. ("Look! Here I am going through the Jewish process of purification. How can I simultaneously be rejecting Jewish custom?") But these aggressors had no interest in reason. They had either been in Turkey for the violent episodes that had erupted against me, or they saw themselves as having special inside information from back home. When they saw me, their position was "There's the guy everyone knows is guilty!" They acted as if everyone in Jerusalem, and the whole world for that matter, had been searching for me as an escaped convict. Anyway, they got their hands on me and stirred everyone up.

"This is him! This is the man teaching everywhere against our Law!" they shouted.

I couldn't get a word of self-defense in. These Turkish Jews went on to claim I had brought Gentiles into the temple, thus defiling it. This was not at all true. They must have seen the four young men—who were under a Nazarite vow and whom I had brought in with me for the purification rites earlier in the week—and simply assumed they were my Gentile friends. (These young men did not run to my defense; I never saw them again.) The whole city seemed ablaze with anger against me. I was dragged out of the temple, and the gates were slammed shut behind me. I'd been through some rough stuff, but I was convinced that this was my end.

With Jerusalem under Roman rule, Roman soldiers were stationed in the city. The Roman watch saw the chaos, and in no time soldiers were everywhere. Even the Roman tribune was there. Together, their presence stopped my immediate beating but didn't otherwise settle the crowd, who were so worked up that they didn't think a minute about the very real threat of the Roman force.

The tribune ordered my arrest, but the crowd was so loud, still shouting out a mixture of accusations and general abuse at me, that the tribune couldn't hear above the cacophony. He ordered me taken back to the barracks for questioning. When we got to the steps, the soldiers had to carry me up them; the crowd had gotten so violent that it was easier to carry me than to protect me as I walked.

I asked the tribune if I could say something to him, but when he heard that I spoke Greek, he wasn't interested in my request. Greek wasn't at all uncommon, but he'd expected me to speak Aramaic like most of the Jews in the city. The jolt of surprise sent his mind looking for an explanation as to why I would be speaking Greek, so his mind went to the one thing that it had been dwelling on of late. Some Greek-speaking Egyptian had recently stirred up a revolt of four thousand men, whom he had led out into the wilderness in preparation for attack. The Romans had shattered this revolt without any real difficulty, but the leader had escaped. Associating the chaos with my Greek tongue, the tribune thought that maybe I was this Egyptian. I told him that I was just a Jew from Tarsus and begged him for the chance to speak to the people.

I was surprised when the tribune granted my request. I suppose he thought it was worth seeing if I could calm the situation. Or, maybe, he expected me to instigate the crowd against Rome, which would let him wipe the whole mess clean with his sword. I motioned for quiet, and a great hush quickly smothered the noise. I raised my voice and spoke to the crowd in Aramaic, the common language of the Jerusalem Jews. Upon hearing their native tongue, they gave their full attention.

"I am a Jew!" I shouted. "Born in Tarsus but educated in our Jewish Law here in Jerusalem where I was zealous for our God. Being deluded and thinking it our God's will, I persecuted the Christians here, and I persecuted them hard. I asked for and was given a letter from your high priest and the council, granting me authority to press the persecution into Damascus. Just ask them. They'll say it's true." I hoped that my background would score credibility with some.

I then related the story of my turning to Christ. I didn't leave out any of the details, nor did I embellish any part, but explained everything clearly and truthfully. Stories make the best explanations, so I went through my story step by step: the blinding light, the voice of our Lord Jesus, my mission…

But then, when I told them that the Lord sent me to the Gentiles, they lost it. The quiet was broken as if by a sudden clap of thunder from the crowd. The noise was tremendous, making it difficult to hear actual words, but their message was clear: "Take Paul away, not to prison, but to death!" After everything I had said going over so well, I should have left out the reference to the Gentiles; it was the idea that our God would send me to the non-Jews that had tipped them over the edge.

Not only did disorder erupt from their shouting, but disorder seemed to be their goal. As they shouted, many of them took off their cloaks and thrashed them against the ground to fling dust into the air. The Roman tribune was disgusted, not to mention thoroughly annoyed, by the scene. Romans live to act decisively; the figuring-it-out part annoys them. This Roman tribune had hoped that letting me speak would at least clarify the situation so he could act decisively, but all he had heard was a bunch of Jewish religious stuff, the result of which was completely bewildering to him.

He ordered me to be taken to the barracks for a flogging. Perhaps that would get him a clear and concise answer about the meaning of all this Jewish fuss. The centurion stretched me out, all tied up for the whip, but before the first blow found my back, I calmly but with a raised voice asked the centurion if it was lawful to flog a Roman citizen who had not received a trial. My question had its desired effect, giving my would-be whipper the jitters. They had never dreamed that I was a Roman citizen with all the accompanying privileges.

The centurion called the tribune, who asked me if I was indeed a Roman citizen. I told him that I was, putting the jitters into him too.

"I paid a lot of money for my citizenship," he informed me, somewhat skeptical that I was part of his semi-elite circle of fellow citizens. I calmly told him that I was a citizen by birth, which was the truth, and he didn't press any further.

The Romans withdrew flogging from their intent, but they did not release me from confinement. Had they pushed me out, there can be little doubt that I would have been torn to pieces by that mob. I spent the night safely in prison.

The next day, the tribune was still confused. Why the Jews would lose their minds because some god had sent me to talk to Gentiles completely baffled him. He took me down before the Jewish court, the chief priest, and the council, hoping for answers.

Before the Jewish Court: The High Priest

Standing before the Jewish court, I didn't shrink from looking them right in the eyes. I stated quite firmly that I had lived my life to keep my conscience clear before God, right up to that very day. That's all I had to say for the high priest to order the Jew standing closest to me to strike me in the mouth, and he did so.

Contrary to how it may seem based on my past, I do not enjoy being hit. It hurt. I was frustrated and sick of it. I called the high priest a hypocrite and threatened that God was going to strike *him*. Then I asked him sharply if he was really going to pretend to judge me according to the Law when he was so eager to step outside of the Law by striking me.

Feigning shock and indignation, the man who had hit me asked if I was really so bold as to speak rudely to the high priest. I responded loudly that I didn't know he was the high priest and that I would not have spoken so if I had.

The first edge of this sword cut with the fact that our Lord and Savior Jesus Christ, not this poser, is the true High Priest. Jesus's claim on the position has superseded and nullified all other claims; there is no other with the authority of the High Priest. This point, however, passed without notice, as expected.

The second edge of the sword, however, sliced into its mark. It was a direct assault on the high priest's claim to authority, even if Christ hadn't come.

The reason is historical. Scripture plainly appointed Aaron as the original high priest shortly after the Israelites' exodus from Egypt. From there, we should be able to trace an unbroken line right down to the present high priest, but we can't. Antiochus IV, the "Little Horn" from the Daniel prophecy, broke this line a couple hundred years ago by appointing high priests at his pleasure. Rome later granted the authority to appoint the high priest to the person they had appointed king over the Promised Land: Herod, the very same who tried to have the infant Jesus murdered. Even now, King Agrippa II has the authority to appoint and withdraw the high priest, who is almost always a Sadducee.

Thus, the office of high priest is not filled by the scripturally appropriate family of Aaron's line or even a popularly accepted family. The office of high priest is filled by the whim of our foreign appointed rulers. Even the Sadducees find this distasteful. At least they are deeply embarrassed by the subject.

So, you see, even if our Savior had not yet come, the man dressed up and playing the part of high priest had neither scriptural nor popular authority to hold this office. My simple comment that I didn't know he was the high priest was something they would much rather let slide than discuss. They fidgeted uncomfortably, and instead of asking the obvious question, "How could you possibly not know that this is the high priest?" we simply moved on. I have to admit, it felt nice to punch back a little.

Before the Jewish Court: Sadducees and Pharisees

From my position, I got a good look at the assembly. Ironically, my being on display gave me an ideal vantage point from which to examine them. Taking it in, I realized the assembly was a mix of Sadducees and Pharisees.

Now, Romans and other Gentiles tend to see all Jews as one homogeneous glob of people who all think the same way. To the outside world, we're "the Jews." But, in fact, a great deal of differences and disputes within the Jewish community exist; some of these clashes involve significant theological issues. This was especially true at the time I was expounding the Word of our Lord in Jerusalem.

(Actually, even at that point, those of us who followed the Way didn't see ourselves as having converted to some new religion separate from that of the Jews. It was as though we were Jews who had the next step, a fuller understanding than the other Jews. Of course, as far as what's most important–faith in Jesus Christ–we were more like our Gentile brothers. But as far as everything else—culture, customs, habits, background, and so on—we were still more like the other Jews. We were the Jews whose Messiah had come. When spreading the gospel, I always went to the synagogues first because it seemed the most natural thing to do.)

I was before the Jewish court and in front of the assembly of Sadducees and Pharisees, and I was going to work the theological division between the two groups to my advantage.

Many people like to trace the Pharisees back to an ultra-pious, intellectual group and then blithely associate the Sadducees with a simple social class of the ultra-rich. This isn't exactly fair, and worse, it completely dismisses the most important theological distinction. These two groups are direct opposites on many theological issues and have even disagreed on which books should be considered Scripture.

The Sadducees and Pharisees divide as opposites along intellectual and theological issues. But from these theological differences, the two groups have developed very different social personalities, which are much more apparent to the casual observer. The Sadducees became most comfortable with foreign rule and now consort with the Romans and the Roman-appointed king, which is why they keep getting appointed to the position of high priest. In this age, when the people contemplate a warrior messiah coming to free them from foreign oppression, being a Roman-kiss-up Sadducee is exceedingly unpopular. In fact, at this point, the only thing keeping them from falling into a fringe sect is their relationship with the Romans. Because the Pharisees remain the foil to the Sadducees, they probably get more credit than they deserve as defenders of Jewishness, which gives their theological views a credibility boost.

One of the most fundamental theological divides between these two groups is that the Sadducees believe there will never be a resurrection of the dead, which the Pharisees expect.

It was here, in this great division, that I saw an opportunity to save my skin. I would exploit the resurrection of the dead issue. Of course, as far as they go, the Pharisees are right—the general resurrection of the dead will happen. I had been raised and trained as a Pharisee, and it made complete sense that I would be associated with the Pharisees now, especially on the resurrection issue, not to mention that they, too, believed in angels and the Spirit. Neither group believed in the resurrection of our Lord and Savior Jesus Christ, of course, but I found a little grey area here. After all, faith in Jesus Christ's resurrection was the reason I was there in the first place.

Combine this with my not being too keen on sitting through an orderly farce of a trial sure to end in my execution, and I was inspired to shout out to the assembly, "I am a Pharisee! I am the son of a Pharisee! I am on trial here because I have hope in the resurrection of the dead!" All true, even if not conveying the full details of the story.

This created a violent uproar, but for once, it wasn't directed straight at me. The assembly had divided and chosen sides, Pharisees against Sadducees. They loudly argued their theological divisions, and some of the Pharisee scribes stood up and indignantly stated that there was nothing to be found wrong with me. How funny is that? They asked, "What if an angel has spoken to him?" This was also funny because the Sadducees don't believe in angels either.

This set the atmosphere to near-riot. Just like that, the room went from everyone against me to two large groups yelling their favorite platitudes in the same old debate, though I was still a prominent target for the Sadducees.

I had intended to cause a stir and hoped to shut the court down, but as the Sadducees succeeded in turning more focus back to me, it began to look like I would get shredded. Luckily, the Roman tribune had been watching intently and had ordered soldiers to take me from the assembly by force. They did so, returning me to the safety of the barracks. I have to admit, there is something mildly amusing about having a Roman prison as my safe place.

This must have driven the Roman tribune insane. He had taken me to the Jewish court to learn what was going on only to get more of the same incomprehensible behavior and mystifying theological dispute. By this point, he must have thought the Jews were like children in the toddler stage of life, when reason is useless. For now, I was safely in prison while he tried to figure out how to deal with the situation.

That night, in prison, the Lord came to me. He stood near and told me to take courage. The Lord told me that I was to testify to the facts about Him in Rome just as I had done in Jerusalem. Although there seemed to be quite a challenge in front of me, I was comforted by the knowledge that I would at least live long enough to be an even more useful tool for the Lord.

The next day, my nephew came to me in the prison with disturbing news. He told me that forty of the local Jews had made a vow to neither eat nor drink until they killed me. This group of conspirators told the chief priest and the Jewish elders of their vow and requested their help. The chief priest and elders were to send for the Roman tribune and request that I be taken back down to them, as if they wanted more information to better decide the case against me. The forty conspirators, for their part, would ensure that I never made it all the way; they would kill me in transit. This would be a very bold move, considering that they would have to get past Roman guards to accomplish their task.

I called to the Roman centurion and told him to take my nephew to the Roman tribune. I explained only that my nephew had something to tell the tribune, but a combination of my demeanor and the atmosphere surrounding my situation conveyed the importance of the message to the centurion. He escorted my nephew off without question.

Many hours passed before I knew of the preparations that were being made or even that my nephew had been allowed to speak to the tribune, for that matter. That night, however, at about nine o'clock, I was on a horse, riding swiftly with what seemed to be a small army. The Roman tribune had quietly arranged to send me and my traveling party off. I was being transferred to go before Governor Felix in Caesarea. The tribune had found that the best way to deal with my situation was to pass the buck up a level and let the governor figure it out. We stopped partway that night, and in the morning, most of the small army returned to Jerusalem. About seventy horsemen, however, continued to Caesarea as my protection.

Caesarea

In Caesarea, the soldiers presented me, along with a letter from the Roman tribune, to Felix, the governor for this province of the Roman Empire. Much later, Felix let me see the letter, so I can tell you its message:

This Paul had been seized by the Jews who were about to kill him in a near-riot atmosphere. I am still baffled by the situation. I took Paul before the Jewish council to learn the charges, but I'm still in the dark. It's just Jewish stuff, I'm sure of that, but I can't figure out what the issue is, except that they're all idiots.

(Maybe this is what had amused Felix enough to want to show me the letter.)

The letter continued:

He definitely didn't do anything to deserve death or even imprisonment under Roman law. I sent him to you when I learned of a conspiracy to kill him here; the maintenance of order, which you'll agree is in both of our best interests, demanded his transfer. If the Jews had succeeded in attacking the Roman troops transporting this Paul, there is no telling how the situation could have escalated. Thus, I send him to you. By the time you read this, I will have informed his accusers of his transfer and instructed them to also go to you if they intend to press their grievance, whatever it may be.

After having read the letter in its entirety, Roman Governor Felix looked mildly annoyed. He asked me gruffly what province I was from. When I answered, he knew that my case was clearly in his jurisdiction and that he had no chance of bouncing me out for someone else to deal with. So he acquiesced to hearing the case once my accusers arrived. Until then, he sent me to one of his palaces, where I was under guard. Technically, I was imprisoned, but practically, it wasn't bad at all.

Under Felix

I had made it to Caesarea in only two days. It took my accusers five. Perhaps they needed some extra time to prepare when they realized there was to be a real trial. They even brought a professional lawyer to press their persecution.

Their lawyer started: "Oh, Felix, most excellent Felix! Great reformer! We Jews accept your reforms with gratitude, everywhere and always! Your reforms come straight from your brilliant foresight, you magnificent man, you. Because of you, we enjoy peace. I beg you to be kind and hear us, only briefly."

I could have gagged. The Jews hated Felix, Governor of Bribe Taking. He had been governor for perhaps the least peaceful term of any Roman governor up to that point. Still, this lawyer worked his flattery as hard as he could. And it did seem to please Felix, a master of self-delusion who wanted to believe every word of it.

Finally, after so massaging the governor, the lawyer got down to it. He described me as a plague infecting the Jewish world: "This Paul leads the cult-sect sometimes called Nazarenes. He stirs up riots every chance he gets. We were able to endure no more when he tried to profane the Temple, and only then did we seize him. Question him directly, and he'll tell you everything we accuse him of is true," said the lawyer.

Here at last, my accusers gave me something solid I could address directly. There were three main points to hit: one, that I do follow Jesus Christ; two, that I don't incite riots; and three, that I never profaned the Temple.

I responded formally when Governor Felix nodded at me to speak. I started with the customary deference to authority that the Romans so love: "I happily make my defense before you, as you've judged in this land for many years." It was true; Felix had been governor, thus acting as a judge, of the province for five or six years by that time. So I was able to meet the flattery custom of the Roman courts without pretending that this less-than-mediocre governor was a great man. Though, admittedly, Felix seemed much less pleased with my introduction than that of the flatterer.

I went on, "Yes, I *am* a follower of Jesus of Nazareth and have faith in Him. And I *am* a leader within that community." I started my defense. I went on to admit that, even then, I did have hope that my accusers would turn to Jesus. But I also made it clear that I worshiped the God of the Jews, the God of our fathers, and that I believed the Law and the prophets. In short, not only was I a follower of Jesus Christ, but I was also a faithful Jew.

"I am not at all responsible for starting riots and have never profaned the Temple. When I did go into the Temple, I was there for purification, attending to myself and the four young men I had come in with. Who thinks they can go to the Temple for purification while callously profaning the sacred place?" I pointed out that my accusers couldn't prove I had done anything wrong. They had erupted into a mob all by themselves and only after they had found me minding my own business. There was no crowd or tumult when they first grabbed me. How can my simple, peaceful existence be enough to bring a charge of riot-inciting against me? I had only come to Jerusalem, bringing alms to my people, and gone to the Temple for purification.

I nailed every point and continued, "Some Jews from Asia—who, by the way, ought to be here to accuse me directly since they were the ones who stirred up the problem in the first place—they grabbed me and took me before the Jewish council for my beliefs. Even though they should be the ones pressing the case, let my accusers who are here speak again. Ask them *exactly* what I did wrong, how I stirred up a riot, or how I profaned the Temple. The only thing they'll be able to say is that while before the council, I yelled out, 'I'm on trial because I believe in the resurrection of the dead.'" How could my accusers deny that I was on trial simply for believing in Jesus Christ? They couldn't.

The outcome? Felix, in all his magisterial ineptitude, simply put off deciding the case. Clearly, he knew I was innocent and should be freed, but he held out hope that a cash bribe for my release would be forthcoming. So he held me, which wasn't all that bad. I was in custody but given a fair amount of liberty. Plus, my guards were ordered to let my friends come in to see me and attend to my needs. (Though it's more likely that they were allowed to come because Felix hoped they would pool money to bribe him with.) Plus, while in Roman custody, I wasn't available for the Jews to kill.

After a few days, Felix sent for me to speak to him and his wife, whom he had wedded in scandal. (Through his deceit, Felix had managed to bring about her divorce from her first husband—maybe everyday stuff for the Roman elite, but not the best way to endear yourself to the Jewish people.) At the time, I thought they were interested in the Way of Jesus Christ. Much to his dismay, I didn't soften and tailor the Word to his pleasure or grant him a flattery fix. When I really started to get into the topics of righteousness, self-control, and the coming judgment, Felix grew more and more agitated until he sent me away, saying, "for the present," as if he had enjoyed my speaking but something else more important had come up. He told me that he would call for me when he got a chance, and he did call for me often. (It was during this time that Felix showed me the letter the Roman tribune had sent to Caesarea with me.) Unfortunately, I don't think I made any headway teaching him the Word. I was quickly sent away "for the present" whenever I discussed proper living or retribution. I can only assume his regular calls were more intended as invitations for me to offer him a bribe than to hear anything I had to say.

Two years passed like this. I was safe but unable to preach, except, of course, to Felix and those who came to me. I could no longer seek new people to bring into the Way and thus do my duty to build the body of Christ. When I learned that Felix was to be replaced with a new Roman governor, Governor Festus, I expected that he would finally set me free. Felix had proven his incapacity to deal with and maintain peace between the Jews and Gentiles in his jurisdiction, and so Rome removed him from office. It was clear to everyone, probably even to my accusers, that I was innocent. But ever the politician and crowd-pleaser, Felix left me in prison, thinking it would keep the Jews cool.

For the record, at no time during these two years did I receive word of mass starvation in Jerusalem. Nor was I killed. Apparently, the forty conspirators quietly forgot their vow to not eat or drink until they had killed me.

Under Festus

I was still stuck in Caesarea, technically imprisoned but housed well and allowed visits and provisions from my friends. My situation was much too comfortable for my adversaries' liking. The new Roman governor, Festus, hardly had time to settle into his new position when they were pushing my case at him and urging him to send me to Jerusalem.

Festus went to Jerusalem only three days after he had arrived in his new province. While there, my accusers had said, "Bring Paul here. You can get his case out of the way." But Governor Festus told them he would be in Caesarea soon, so there was no need to have me transported to Jerusalem. This wasn't what my adversaries, who planned to kill me in transit, wanted to hear. But they could think of no legitimate reason to press the issue harder.

The day after he arrived in Caesarea, Festus took his seat on the tribunal and had me brought before him. My accusers were with him, ready to press serious albeit unsound charges against me. I have to admit, it still didn't look good for me. Yes, it was clear that I was fully innocent of any wrongdoing, but my judge, Governor Festus, had spent the previous eight to ten days with them, soaking in their lobbying efforts against me. He had even traveled with them from Jerusalem to Caesarea. The scales seemed heavily weighted against me.

My adversaries pressed their empty case, and I had my chance to speak. Festus looked somewhat surprised by my defense and my adversaries' inability to prove my guilt. It was clear that the nuances of their charges had shifted somewhat from how they'd been portraying the situation to him while advocating my death.

Festus's mind functioned as cutthroat as any Roman political climber, so the clarity of my complete innocence alerted him that a fair trial wasn't my adversaries' goal; they wanted me out of the way. As brand-new governor, Festus was willing to play some political games to win favor but hesitated to make an obviously wrong judgment in my case. Steps of corruption could make him rich, but one leap of corruption could cause his fall. Festus now saw the convenience of handing me over to my accusers on a pretext.

Trying to regain his missed opportunity, Festus asked me, "Would you like to go to Jerusalem to be tried there instead?" Wouldn't that have been nice for him? He wouldn't have to order an obviously innocent man to be killed, and I'd still get whacked. Everyone's problem—me—would be solved.

The glitch in this plan was that there was no legal reason to send me off for trial elsewhere. That's why he'd asked me. I guess he had hoped I didn't know the situation and would therefore rather be tried "back home," so to speak. I refused the offer. I hadn't broken the law of the Jews. I hadn't broken the law of the Temple. I hadn't broken Caesar's law. I had no intention of going to Jerusalem for an ambush party to be thrown in my honor.

So I told Festus, "I am before Caesar's tribunal, which is the proper court for me to be tried in. You know I have done no wrong to the Jews. I wouldn't try to escape my punishment, even death, if I deserved it. But if you don't find me guilty, you have no right to give me over to them. I appeal to Caesar." In technical legal terms, I appealed the case to a higher court—the highest court of Rome.

Festus conferred with his counsel, but when it came right down to it, he didn't want to deal with me any more than Governor Felix had. He accepted my appeal to go before Caesar, eager to push the conflict between me and my Jewish adversaries off as someone else's problem.

I hadn't really thought it through before blurting out, "I appeal to Caesar!" To be honest, I did really like the dramatic effect of the moment. Now that the appeal was granted, however, I became sincerely excited at the prospect of taking the gospel before Emperor Nero's court.

Agrippa II

After my appeal was granted, I was back in custody awaiting my shipment to Rome for trial before Caesar. A few days later, Agrippa II, the king, arrived in town with his half-sister. They were staying in Caesarea as Roman Governor Festus's houseguests.

First, I want to be clear that I am not willing to fall into gossip about Agrippa's relationship with his sister. Of course, along with their obviously inappropriate relationship regularly displayed in public, much more direct and crude rumors abound from places they've stayed. I won't get into any of that, but knowing the rumors, I'll admit that her presence gave me a little shock of embarrassment.

Second, don't let the "king" thing fool you; Agrippa was firmly under the Roman thumb. The king is little more than another governor for Rome. Sometimes Rome places this pseudo-king in control over more of the Promised Land, sometimes over less, but the title requires the express approval of the emperor and the senate and has nothing to do with the historical line of kings going back to King David.

Because this kingship has basically been in the same family since the Romans came to power, it looks hereditary to the outside world. It is not. While it looks like the kingship has gone from father to son to nephew to son, it has technically gone from Rome to father, from Rome to son, from Rome to nephew, and from Rome to son. It isn't a dynasty at all. It has only stayed in the same family because Rome chose to keep it in the same family, giving the appearance of a dynasty.

This Roman-appointed line was made up of four generations, each with Herod in his name. This has caused endless confusion for people outside the Jewish world:

Herod the Great: His ascension to power was messy, but when Augustus was emperor of Rome *(as of 30 BC),* he confirmed Herod in his position as king. This Herod ordered the mass slaughter of infants in an attempt to kill the baby Jesus, the coming Messiah whom Herod feared would threaten his kingship.

Herod's son Herod Antipas: Herod Antipas governed during Jesus's lifetime. He received the governorship of the lands of Galilee, where Jesus Christ came from, and Perea, where John the Baptist's following grew. However, he never received the title "king" and ruled only about a fourth of what had been his father's kingdom. (Making Antipas the second generation of the Herodian line is really a bit of a cheat used to help Christians keep track of the Herods who are most relevant for their story; for world politics at the time, he was not the most important son of Herod the Great.)

John the Baptist condemned Herod Antipas's inappropriate marriage without reserve, and there were a lot of people listening to John, so Antipas had him arrested. At a party, Antipas had John's head brought on a platter because he wanted to honor the request from a girl who had danced so very well that he just had to reward her with anything she wanted. And she wanted John the Baptist's head on a platter.

When Jesus was under Pilate's control, Pilate sent him to see Antipas, who was delighted because he had heard much about Jesus and hoped to see a miracle. Not only did Jesus fail to perform, but he also did not answer the many questions Antipas put to him. The brief episode ended with Antipas and his soldiers making fun of Jesus, dressing him in an elegant robe to further mock him, and then sending him back to Pilate.

Herod Agrippa I: He was the third generation of the Herodian line but represented a zig-zag in that line. He was the grandson of Herod the Great but the nephew of Herod Antipas. This was the Herod Agrippa who had James, the brother of John, killed and Peter arrested in Jerusalem.

So Christianity's relationship with the Herodian kingship has never been stellar. But now we come to Herod Agrippa I's son, the Herod before whom I was to appear.

Herod Agrippa II was only seventeen when his father died *(AD 44)*. Emperor Claudius eventually gave him the title of king and the governorship of a small area too far north to matter much to most Jews. At the same time, the Roman procurators, or governors, were installed over the rest of the Promised Land, including Judea. This is how the situation came to be, with Agrippa II, the king who wasn't actually king over the land of the Jews, and Roman Procurator-Governor Festus, who was charged with ruling over Judea, Samaria, and Perea. Both were fully subject to Roman rule.

Agrippa II also had a thoroughly Roman background, having been educated there, and his friendships with Emperor Claudius and Emperor Nero made his the most sought-after association that any politically motivated governor could want to have. But Agrippa II's disposition was softer than that of his predecessors. He was subservient to his Roman superiors, but he lacked that truly sniveling quality only the greatest political competence can master. He seemed to have a real affection for the Romans. He also had a softer hand dealing with the Jews. All the same, he fully understood that his job was to keep them in line.

Anyone could find this political and subservient kingship distasteful, but the Jewish people find it all the more disdainful since the concept of the Messiah eclipses it. The Messiah would be the savior of the Jewish people, but "savior" has always been interpreted as a military leader "saving" or delivering the people from a foreign military power that would occupy or otherwise controlled Israel.

The Messiah, who, according to the Prophets, would be the hereditary heir of God's anointed King David, would rise up and militarily drive off our Gentile overlords. The coming of the Messiah was to be the return of the "King of the Jews" and the return of the kingship to the proper family line. This concept, which had been popular enough among the Jews when they were under the Greek rulers, only gained momentum under the Roman rulers and the Jewish kings who were neither of the Davidic line, nor popularly supported, nor even really kings.

These Jewish kings, however, were aware of this threat; hence, Herod the Great's decision to slay the infants.

Belief that Jesus was the Messiah had long since ceased causing any anxiety to Agrippa II, if it ever had. Especially before His death, Jesus was sometimes grouped together with the many revolutionaries who popped up claiming to be the Messiah. But when the authorities came to understand that the Christians' Messiah brought non-military, non-violent salvation from eternal death, they brushed it off as harmless and, therefore, unimportant.

Unlike his father, who had still been concerned that Jesus's followers might stir up revolution even after their leader's death, Agrippa II could view me with a lighthearted demeanor as a worshiper of a confused, not to mention dead, messiah who had no interest in his crown.

Before Agrippa II

Roman Governor Festus set up a mock trial so that Agrippa II and his sister Bernice could hear my case. This trial was really only a social event posing as official business, as my case had already been ruled upon and my appeal granted, but Agrippa certainly knew how to play king. Not many men, Roman or otherwise, could outdo Agrippa when it came to splendor. For this event, the flashy king played the part of fake importance perfectly.

Agrippa and Bernice entered the audience hall with over-the-top pomp and display. Military tribunes and prominent men of the city sat with them. Then I was hauled in before them. Festus was the first to speak. He addressed the entire crowd, especially his guests.

"This is Paul, a man who has set the entire Jewish community to petition me and clamor for his death. When his case came before me, I understood only that the Jews say a man named Jesus died. But Paul says this Jesus is alive. I heard nothing in the case to suggest that he deserves the punishment of death, but I didn't know how to investigate the matter further. I asked him if he wanted to go to Jerusalem to be tried there, but he appealed to the emperor. I decided to accept his appeal and send him. Today, we are gathered so that you may hear his case. I have no idea what to write to Caesar regarding this situation. Perhaps you can help me decide how to phrase the document regarding Paul's appeal," Festus finished. And I once more had an opportunity to proclaim the gospel.

If Agrippa and Festus wanted to pretend this social event was a trial, so be it. I would pretend that my evangelizing was part of the trial. I held out my arms and addressed my "defense" to Agrippa. I followed the normal formula and started with praise, telling him I felt glad to be able to speak before him. I, in fact, was delighted to have another major platform from which to pronounce the gospel. But I was also happy to be before Agrippa because he had a solid understanding of the customs and controversies among us Jews. I begged him to listen patiently, knowing he would understand if only he paid me some attention.

"King Agrippa," I began. "I was raised in Jerusalem, and all the Jews know I have lived my life as a Pharisee, the strictest group of Jews." I wanted him to understand that my faith in Jesus

Christ wasn't just a pretense I invoked to get out of following the Jewish Law. This had been an important selling point when I was evangelizing for Christ, as it helped to build my credibility with those I was trying to convert. I hoped it would also build my credibility with Agrippa.

My history as a Pharisee was more relevant here than just credibility, though. Agrippa understood that as a Pharisee, I believed in the resurrection of the dead. He would also understand how vehemently the Sadducee Jews would oppose me for this belief. So, establishing my alignment with the Pharisee Jews, I told Agrippa that it was my belief in this resurrection of the dead that had landed me before him. Soon, he would see where the Pharisees and I parted ways in that they still waited for what I knew to have come to pass.

I told Agrippa of my having persecuted the Christians, my encountering Jesus on the road to Damascus, and that, leading up to the encounter, I had been acting on the high priest's authority. This highlighted for him that the Jews had been persecuting Christians strictly based on doctrinal belief, not for inciting riots or defiling temples.

I explained to Agrippa that Jesus commissioned me to turn the people, Jew and Gentile alike, away from darkness and death to His light—from under Satan's thumb into God's caring hands. I explained that by doing so, they would receive forgiveness from God and would be sanctified by faith in Him. It's not about what believers *do* but about the grace God bestows upon them. Thus, I had begun to evangelize, none too subtly, for Jesus Christ to Agrippa and to all those present.

I told the king that from the moment I had received my epiphany and instructions from the Lord, I acted in obedience. That is, I obeyed God. "I preached for God in Damascus, in Jerusalem, throughout the region around Jerusalem, and directly to the Gentiles," I told him. "I did all I could to convince everyone I met to repent and turn to God. I told them to repent and then act in accord with their repentance, being careful not to backslide." Then I told the simple truth, that it was for this reason that the Jews, Pharisee and Sadducee alike, had seized me and attempted to kill me.

I pointed out to Agrippa that against all challenges, God had kept me alive even if not always out of harm's way. "Look," I said, "I'm only saying what Moses and the prophets said would come to pass, that the Christ must suffer, die, and rise from the dead. He would proclaim the light of His message to both Jews and Gentiles. And it has come to pass! The Christ suffered, died, was buried, and rose again in fulfillment of the Scriptures. And now His Word spreads to Jew and Gentile alike."

As I spoke, the attention of those in the hall seemed to grow increasingly focused. Then, as if he had caught himself being pulled into the Way, Festus blurted out in a voice of exaggerated amusement, "Paul, you're out of your mind!" And with a great, all-in-good-fun smile, he told me that my education had taught me out of my skull.

I very politely told Festus that not only was I sane but also speaking rationally. I was speaking the Truth. Then I made a bit of a tactical move: I told Festus in no uncertain terms that Agrippa must have been aware of the things I was talking about.

After all, none of it was done in secret. I was directly addressing Festus, but my words were intended for Agrippa. I wasn't some lone nutcase expounding my own doctrines. I was proclaiming the gospel of Jesus Christ, which he already knew was spreading throughout the Jewish world. I rhetorically asked Agrippa if he believed in the words of the prophets and quickly answered the question for him so he wouldn't feel put on the spot. "I know that you believe!" I said.

Agrippa listened attentively and, I am convinced, felt that warm pull to the Way. But he caught himself just in time to dodge salvation. In a flash, he realized that he, the reason for all the pomp in the hall, would look silly in the eyes of many men if he were to lend credibility to the Way.

Taking his cue from Festus, Agrippa answered me in a jocular voice, "Paul, with the way you talk, it wouldn't take you long at all to convince me to join the Christians!"

Emphasizing the sincerity in my voice, I told Agrippa that I wholeheartedly wished not only that he turn to Christ Jesus but that all who heard me speak turn as well. From small to great, all are welcome in Him. And that was that; the show was over. My statement had flustered them with discomfort, so they hastened to close up shop.

When they rose and withdrew from the hall, the grandeur seemed deflated. It was as if they held an armload of shiny things but sat watching the salvation boat sail off to the horizon, knowing that they had missed it and knowing that they wouldn't board even if it were to return. Still, none of them showed any outward signs of anger to me, and I found this a nice change from what I had grown accustomed to. In fact, they seemed unanimous in the belief that I deserved neither imprisonment nor death. Agrippa even went as far as to tell Festus that I could have been set free if my trial hadn't been definitively ruled on with the granting of my formal appeal to Caesar.

I can't say I was heartbroken about this, though, since being set free would almost certainly have meant death for me in fulfillment of some conspiracy. More importantly, I knew God's plan for me would take me to Rome. Since Festus's ruling, I had some clarity of how He intended to get me there.

Shipped Off and Shipwrecked

The tumult settled down as Festus settled in as governor. I was back under guard, waiting to be shipped to Rome. I had been stuck in Caesarea for about two years, largely neglected by the Roman system of government. But once the weather turned harsh, making it the worst time of year for sea travel, I was shipped off to Italy. Ah, bureaucracy. A Roman centurion, Julius, took charge of me for my transfer.

Together with some other prisoners, I was placed on a small ship not designed for open sea travel. But we coasted along, never leaving sight of land, until we reached a larger port city where we transferred into a more seaworthy vessel. The weather, however, would try to prove the ship insufficient for the journey.

Julius treated me very well, especially for a prisoner. In fact, I was allowed to visit and stay with my friends, my brothers and sisters in Christ, when we stopped for the night in another port city. It was only one night, but it was a nice break from the rough travel.

Out of respect for Julius, and in thanks for the bit of freedom he provided me, I made sure to be on the ship early the next day. In stark contrast to my pleasant evening the night before, I was now back on the boat getting hammered by a strong wind. The wind was so bad that we sailed the other way around Cyprus to use the island itself as a windbreaker. Considering the conditions, the otherwise silly route did provide some relief from the harshest winds. Once past Cyprus, though, it was back to the mercy of the tempest blasts on the open sea.

We stopped at another port city and transferred ships again. This time, Julius found a ship bound for Italy to put us on. We seemed to be bobbling around a lot, so some of the other prisoners quietly questioned Julius's competence to get us to Rome. But I gave him the benefit of the doubt. I assumed our options were severely limited by the time of year and weather; there were simply fewer vessels willing to sail. Additionally, Julius probably had more information than I had, or at least, I could not have done a better job of getting us to Rome given the circumstances. Regardless, I had no say in the matter as a prisoner, so although the trip grew frustrating, it was best to recognize that God was in control, and Julius was in charge.

The wind and waves battered us around like a child rolling a small ball from hand to hand, blowing us completely off our course to Rome. Eventually, we sought shelter and harbored on the south side of Crete. It had not been a productive journey.

If the weather was poor when we started out, it had now grown significantly worse. Having left so late in the season and then losing so much time at sea, we crossed into that time of year when there is almost no sea voyage because it's foolishly dangerous. The danger of sailing at this time of year was universally known, and even if you hadn't known the danger, one look at the sky would have warned you not to set sail. Without any divine inspiration whatsoever, I humbly warned Julius that we couldn't make the trip without losing the cargo, the ship, and our lives. Staying put seemed like a no-brainer.

Julius, however, chose to exercise that great Roman virtue: knowing one's place and deferring to superiors. The ship's captain and the owner wanted the ship to sail, so sail it would. And if the ship was going to sail, we were going to be on it. In fairness to them, the harbor wasn't fit to winter the boat, so their decision to push back out into the violent sea and make for Italy wasn't completely nonsensical. Still, risking our lives so the boat could have a cozy winter home wouldn't have been my first choice.

When the wind settled down from insanely dangerous to wildly dangerous, we set sail, racing for Italy. We'd barely cleared the harbor when the violent, whirling winds whipped up to their earlier status of insanely dangerous. We didn't even try to fight those dominating winds for long; we let them drive us along at their will and God's purpose. The ship's little rowboat almost broke free in the chaos. Securing it was very difficult and would later prove to be a wasted effort. The wind continued to push us around as it pleased.

The next day was no better. For safety, we decided to lighten the ship's load by tossing some of the cargo overboard. We were violently beaten around for the rest of the day, and the day after that we tossed some of the ship's heavy equipment to the sea. It wasn't a good situation but better to lose part of the ship than all of it. Day after day, we saw neither sun nor stars; we had nothing to navigate by. But what did it matter? Even if we knew which way we wanted to go, we couldn't fight that storm. Almost everyone gave up all hope of being saved.

Then, sometime during that night of many days, an angel of God stood before me. The angel told me that I would make it to Rome and that the crew would all live; only the ship would be lost. I had let the earlier promise that I would make it to Rome fall to the back of my mind and, in consequence, had grown dejected. The great relief that this angel's message brought me helped to ease the embarrassment I felt for this temporary slip in faith. I was greatly relieved and eager to convey the message to the ship's crew.

Though we hadn't eaten for a long time when I stood before the crew, my faith in God and my delight in His message gave me strength. "Listen, everyone!" I called out. "You should have paid attention to me before we left Crete." I couldn't resist pointing this out. "But as for now, be encouraged as I am! An angel of God has given me cheering words. This ship will go down, but we will all live!" And I knew it would be just as God had promised; the ship would break apart, but we would all be miraculously saved, one way or another.

Lack of sun had made it difficult to keep track of time, but we had been beaten around at sea for about fourteen days. Now we were nearing land. The crew measured the depth of the water at twenty fathoms deep. After letting some time pass, we measured again. This time, the water was only fifteen fathoms deep. We *were* nearing land! It sounded great after a fortnight lost at sea, but then we had a new concern: being smashed against the rocks. We lowered the four anchors attached to the back of the ship and prayed for day's light.

Fear of the rocks encouraged a small group of the sailors to lower the ship's rowboat down into the sea. I'm not sure why they thought using the tiny vessel made a good plan in the onslaught of such weather, but they were looking to cut and run. They said they were going to manually lower the anchors attached to the front of the ship for even more security as only the rear anchors were down at that time. But it was clear that they were just trying to escape the doomed ship. I warned the centurion and the soldiers that everyone would die unless the rowboat thieves stayed on board. I felt inspired to say this and was sure it was true, but I don't really know how I knew. The soldiers quickly cut the ropes to the empty rowboat, which we had worked so hard to secure, and let the storm rip it away.

Just before dawn, I urged the crew to eat. It was time to take some food for strength after a fortnight of eating very little. I took bread, gave thanks to God loudly and clearly so that all might hear, broke it, and began to eat. The entire 276-person crew was encouraged and joined me in the meal. Once we had eaten our fill, we tossed the rest of the wheat overboard. Theoretically, the lighter we were, the higher the boat would float on the water. Therefore, the more we threw overboard, the closer to shore we would get before the ship's bottom would hit ground and bring us to a scraping stop.

Not long after daybreak, we noticed a bay with a promising beach. We had lowered the anchors when we were more afraid of crashing against rocks than hopeful of finding any beach to drive the ship up and onto. Now that we could see the inviting beach, hope overpowered our fear, so we cut the anchors free, leaving them in the water. We hoisted the sail and put the rudder back in place so that we could steer. (We had pulled it out of the water and secured it during our fourteen-day float). We hoped that we could run the ship ashore, so we pushed it as hard as we could.

With all eyes on the shore, we moved forward until–CRASH! The ship stopped quickly, but our bodies did not. The masses of our bodies were hurled forward, leaving no one standing. The ship had crashed into a reef or a sandbar, I'm not sure which. The front of the ship was stuck tight, and the back of the ship, severely damaged in the crash, was being ripped to pieces by the waves.

This would probably have been stressful enough for most people, but I quickly realized something that made the situation worse. Roman soldiers were ever afraid that prisoners would escape. Under Roman law, the soldiers would have been responsible for any escapees. Our present situation presented a perfect opportunity for an escape attempt to anyone bold enough to give it a go. Thus, to avert this risk, the soldiers decided to kill us.

Luckily, Julius wanted to prevent my death, and so he halted the soldiers' plans. Orders were given that all who could swim were to jump into the water. All those who could not swim were to make for shore holding planks and pieces of wood from the breaking-up ship.

We all made it to shore with our lungs still pumping air.

Malta: The Snake

Some of us were more beat up than others, but none were critically injured. We felt relief, but that type of relief that only comes with sheer exhaustion and significant soreness. We had no idea where we were until some locals, clearly untouched by Greek culture, came out to meet us. We were in Malta.

Maltese people were not known as being overly friendly, but they showed us much more kindness than the stereotype suggested we should expect. Perhaps we just looked too pathetic to act aggressively toward. They even started a fire to comfort us when it started to rain and grow cold. Overall, it was as pleasant a welcome as we could hope for.

When the initial blaze of the fire settled down, I picked up a bundle of sticks, found the ideal spot for it on the low-burning coals, and set it down gently. Before I had pulled my hand away, a viper shot out of the bundle and plunged its fangs into my hand. I recoiled my hand, snapping it back to my body as if it were on a spring. The snake hung from my hand, fastened tight.

The Maltese people who were with us gazed at my new predicament and concluded that I must have been a murderer. They reasoned that I may have escaped from the sea, but justice was inescapable; it would finally overtake me through the venom of the snake. As the islanders gazed at me and my new attachment, I violently shook my hand at the fire, breaking the snake's hold. It flipped awkwardly through the air and into the flame, where it writhed and was consumed.

The experience was completely unpleasant, especially that icky, creepy feeling I had upon seeing the snake hanging on to my hand, knowing its fangs were lodged deeply in my flesh. But once the little beast stopped writhing in the fire, my concern had been incinerated with it. The Lord had informed me that I would be in Rome, so I knew that I would live at least that long. I wouldn't need an angel to remind me of that again!

The Maltese people watched me intently after I had disposed of the snake. They seemed confused by my nonchalant demeanor as they watched for the snakebite to swell and puss. They waited for me to fall into a sweating, shivering fever and die. They watched me and waited for a long time, as if at a sporting event. But I suffered nothing, so they concluded that I was not, in fact, a murderer but a god. Still, they had more sense than the Athenians. When I insisted that I was not a god, they looked skeptical, but unlike the (theoretically) more sophisticated Greeks, they didn't try to worship or sacrifice to me.

Malta to Rome

Publius, the chief man of the island, kept an estate near our landing site. It didn't take long for him to learn about our crash and invite us in as his guests. He entertained us very hospitably for three days, even though his father was suffering from a fever and dysentery. When I learned of his father's condition, I asked, "Why didn't you tell us sooner?" and demanded to be taken to the afflicted man. I placed my hands on him and prayed, and he was healed through our Lord Jesus Christ.

News of this healing spread over the island with the wind. Soon, swarms of diseased or severely ill islanders sought me out. And through me, the Lord healed them. This brought us great honor with the people, but at every turn, I carefully dispelled any notion that I was a god, explaining that it was *the* God who had healed them.

Now that there was no ship or cargo to push on with, we wintered three months in Malta. We weren't the only foreigners on the island that winter, and the others, knowing better than to gamble against the sea, still had their ships. Centurion Julius made arrangements for us to sail on one of their vessels when the winter weather broke. The Maltese people, whose hospitality had only increased with their thankfulness for the Lord's healing, loaded the vessel with everything we could need before we sailed.

Back on the sea! After such a disastrous trip to Malta, one would think it impossible to board a vessel with joy. But I was eager to be in Rome, and the time had come. Plus, truth be told, there is some sailor in my heart. I was excited to be back on a ship.

This part of our trip was smooth; a three-day stop in Syracuse, a stop in southernmost Italy, a bit more time scooting up the Italian coast, and our boating adventure came to an end. Off the boat, we found brothers in the Way, and, as it wasn't an inconvenience for him, Julius allowed me to stay with them for seven days before we began the 130-mile trek over land to Rome.

When we had made it to within forty miles of the city, a large group of brothers met us. They had come all the way from Rome. This was a little awkward because I, of course, was still a prisoner. This large party appeared out of nowhere to meet us. As the Roman centurion Julius had treated me so well, I very much feared making him look silly or in any way appearing flippant about his authority. I greeted the brothers from Rome heartily and happily, but I also made it quite clear that I was in custody, that I could not stop at my own will, and that no one was to get in our Roman transporters' way.

Julius and I understood each other quite well. I didn't want our transport disturbed because I wanted Christians recognized as peaceful and nonthreatening to Roman society. Julius just wanted our transport to be over and done with and to look competent in the eyes of his superiors, especially after such a journey. We made eye contact, and he nodded his head toward the back of our group. Julius and the soldiers moved the other prisoners on as I lingered in order to fall behind.

From there, we traveled to Rome as two separate groups. Julius marched the prisoners along in orderly fashion, and the believers and I followed a couple hundred yards behind as a big, loose, meandering mass. When a second large group of our Roman brothers greeted us about thirty miles from the city, we simply absorbed them into our mass. I found great joy in being met by so many believers.

Rome

I'd finally made it to Rome, heart of the world. The Jewish community in Rome was a significant minority, and although the Christian community was smaller, it was still considerable.

About a hundred years ago, General Pompey had secured the Holy Land for Rome by defeating Jerusalem in a three-month siege, after which he desecrated the Temple by entering its most holy place *(63 BC)*. From this battle, Pompey took a huge number of Jews to Rome. This increased the size of the Roman Jewish community, which hadn't been significant up to that point.

Later, many Roman Jews, as well as Jews who have frequent business in Rome, were in Jerusalem on the Pentecost following Jesus's resurrection. They saw Peter and the other apostles speaking in tongues; they heard, and many accepted, the gospel of Jesus the Christ. The new Jewish Christians presumably returned to Rome eager to spread and teach the gospel. Also, others probably went to Rome from Jerusalem when driven by that violent persecution in which I had played such a big role.

These people were all, or mostly all, Jewish believers. And when they tried to spread the Word to their fellow Jews, especially in the synagogues, the response was much like it was around the world. Some accepted the gospel, and some simply rolled their eyes at the Christian nutters, but others rejected it with offended cries of "Blasphemy!" The more the church in Rome grew, the more the hostility grew among the offended nonbelievers against the blossoming Church. Eventually, violence and general uproar between the followers of Jesus and the other Jews reached the point of annoyance for the Roman officials, leading Claudius to ban the Jews from the city. It was clear that Claudius didn't pay much, if any, attention to the Christians. The conflict was within the Jewish community, so as far as he was concerned, the Jews were the problem. He banished the Jews from Rome.

(I hate to say it, but if Claudius had made a fair, informed decision, he would have also booted the Gentile Christians. But the Holy Spirit was at work, using Claudius's ignorance to allow at least the Gentile half of the church in Rome to grow.)

When the Jews were banned from Rome, the Gentile Christians, not seeing themselves as at all Jewish, saw no reason to leave town. Claudius achieved his goal of repressing the strife, but he did so by unwittingly choosing the Christian Gentiles as winners.

With the Jews out of the picture, including the Jewish Christians, no one was arguing whether salvation required one to follow Jewish Law. This not only made it less daunting to join the church in Rome, but it also made it more attractive, as much of the repulsive strife among believers had been removed. Under these circumstances, the Gentile church in Rome grew quickly. And because its growth was along these lines, even Roman eyes eventually came to see it as distinct from the Jewish religion. If Christianity was born in Jerusalem and schooled in Antioch, it came into its own in Rome.

Since that time, the decree exiling the Jews had fallen by the wayside. Most of the Roman Jews had returned to their home city to reestablish the again sizable Roman Jewish population.

Two Years in Rome: With the Jews

I was granted a surprising amount of liberty in Rome, too; I stayed under house arrest with a soldier to guard me. House arrest wasn't particularly common in Rome, but it wasn't unheard of either. It didn't make a lot of sense that I was granted such a situation. I probably won't ever know for sure, but I suspect Agrippa II requested my special treatment.

After a few days had passed, and I had gotten a sense of how this house-arrest situation was going to work, I called the leaders of the local Jewish population to me. It was time to evangelize in Rome!

Addressing the Jewish leaders, I said, "I haven't done anything wrong against the Jewish people, against our customs, or against our fathers. Still, the Jerusalem Jews bound me as a prisoner and gave me to the Romans. The Romans heard my case and wanted to set me free; I hadn't done anything to deserve death. But the Jews objected, so I appealed to Caesar and stayed above the fray by not charging my accusers—fellow Jews—of wrongdoing. It just doesn't seem right to bring a fellow Jew into a Roman court, even if they deserve it. I've asked to speak to you because it's only my belief in the Messiah that has brought me here as a prisoner."

Far from being hostile, my audience simply didn't seem interested in what I had to say; I was already old news. The Jewish leaders had all but forgotten any of the details they may have heard regarding my situation, and they claimed they had not received any letters from Jerusalem regarding my arrest. Plus, I got the sense that these Jews of Rome may have thought the happenings on the outskirts of the empire too quaint to warrant their attention.

Although the conflict between Jewish Christians and Jewish nonbelievers had driven the emperor to expel the Jews from Rome, that expulsion had been over a decade before my arrival. When the Jews were pushed out of the city, the Gentile church grew without Jewish influence. The Christian community in Rome came to be clearly distinct from the Jewish community. This helped to soothe the contention by removing it from within the Jewish community. The Christian trouble, from the Jewish perspective, was no longer one that threatened the orthodox Jews from within, but had largely become just another outside influence to be avoided.

All the Jews of Rome, of course, had heard of the "Christian Movement" and knew was frowned upon by orthodox Jews the world over. They were willing to hear anything I could add to the conversation, though, so we set a date for discussion.

On the morning of that appointed day, a great many Jews arrived at my place, and I was excited to talk to them. I used the Law of Moses and the Prophets to try to reason with them and convince them about Jesus. All day long, morning to evening, I testified to the Kingdom of God. A few of my listeners seemed convinced, but most still did not believe. They disagreed and argued amongst themselves as they began to leave.

Less than thrilled with the day's results, I made one last announcement as they left: "The Holy Spirit was right! Through Isaiah, He told your fathers that they would hear but not understand! Let all know, therefore, that the salvation of God has been sent to the Gentiles! They will listen!" With that, the gathering fizzled out, and my ministry to the Roman Jews closed in a completely deflated heap.

My little outburst was more than vented frustration or even a purposeful statement to the Jews. It represented a moment of personal realization for me. Jews the world over had now had a fair crack at salvation. Overwhelmingly, they had rejected Christ. Ever since I was thrown into the Way, I'd never considered it a sect of Judaism. But even though I was an early supporter of bringing Gentiles into the Way and commissioned by God to do so, I saw the followers of Christ as "completed" Jews. After all, Christ fulfilled the Jewish Scriptures. He didn't suffer death and entombment and then rise from the dead just to kick off some new religion.

Now, with this rejection by the Roman Jews, I saw the one true faith as completely outside of Judaism—still open to the Jews, who I assume will always hold a special place in the Lord's heart, but now fully independent of the Jewish religion. If I had sat down and thought about it, I probably would have known better, but before this, it vaguely lingered in the back of my mind that the Jewish faith would naturally transform or become a fulfilled version of itself.

I never excelled when it came to converting my fellow Jews to Christ. Now, this sense of separation came almost as a relief, and I could admit to myself that I hadn't really felt closely connected to the Jewish people for a long time. (Perhaps it had something to do with the repeated attempts on my life.) Peter, on the other hand, had always done much better eliciting positive responses from the Jews. He was also in Rome, in the Jewish section of town.

From time to time, Satan puts seeds of division into the head of a young Christian who has heard an overblown version of the Peter-Paul conflict. Presumably to win my favor, he'll make a snide comment about "Peter the Jew-lover" or the Peter who is "too good to live in the Gentile part of Rome." But they are easily brought down, in love, when they hear my attitude toward God's chosen people and toward the Peter who may be stronger in Christ than anyone else I know.

Plus, it's not like Peter spurned the Gentiles; he just focused on the Jews with whom he had more in common. It only made sense for him to stick closer to what brought the most success for the Church. Rome would prove big enough for both of us to do God's work in our own ways without seeing each other very often.

For two years, I welcomed all who came to me in the house where I was technically under arrest. I proclaimed the Kingdom of God to them and taught them all I could about the Lord Jesus Christ. And still, there was no trial before the emperor.

(The narrative in the biblical book of Acts ends with Paul under arrest in Rome.)

CHAPTER 5:

After Acts

The Same Two Years in Rome: With the Christians

For two years, I welcomed all who came to me in the house where I was technically under arrest. I had decided that I could still be useful to the Lord, even in my position.

When I got to Rome, the Christian situation wasn't anything like what I had expected. I had expected deeply entrenched, factional parties in heated dispute. Perhaps the Corinthians had jaded me. But overall, the Romans were much less devout than the Corinthians. Here, one got the sense they were arguing over which rules their new country club should establish as their norm instead of arguing over fundamental Truth.

The church in Rome, started by some local Jews who had witnessed the Pentecost, had grown without proper guidance. Lack of discernment had become the biggest challenge in Rome. Several conflicting theological doctrines existed within the church, but no one really seemed to see this as a problem. Almost all other local churches had settled down on sound doctrine and had regular communication amongst themselves. Rome, on the other hand, had been a lone satellite, which was ironic since Rome was the center of the secular universe. To bring Rome in line with the other local churches, I had to help establish true doctrine, appoint elders, and make sure it was in regular communication with the other churches.

I had started the process of bringing Rome in line with the other churches by writing a letter to the Romans back when I was in Corinth. The letter had been fairly successful so that by the time I made it to the city, the Romans had already had a chance to clean their own house a bit. The absurd misinterpretation that freedom in Christ must include wild sexual freedom had been cleared up without my presence, along with other, more minor, issues. Those who had been interested in Christianity because they saw it as a chic, new alternative to paganism either came to see the Truth or had left the church.

My time in Rome was nothing near as sensational as my entrance into the city had prepared me to expect. I had arrived with such fanfare—so many people had come many miles from the city just to greet me on my way in—that I anticipated large crowds and major events to become routine. But this celebrity treatment came from my being a celebrity, not from my being an apostle appointed by the Lord to do His work. Everyone had heard of the Paul who could really take a beating for his faith, and they wanted to see him.

My time among the Christians in Rome was much more commonplace. The Romans believed in Jesus Christ and that He had died for their sins so that they could live. So their starting place was solid. My job was to help them retrench in their faith by helping them to replace their misconceptions with sound doctrine. After about a year, it became clear who would make the best leaders, and we commissioned them for the task.

Paul Released

I lingered in Rome, seemingly forgotten by the authorities, for just over two years. Then, my guard—and by this time more of a housemate—abandoned me. He came into my room and told me that his superiors found a "more productive" use for him. Presumably, this meant he wouldn't be replaced.

"That's right," he said. "No one seems to remember or care about you. At least, they don't have any real interest in hearing your case. They are going to quietly forget about you. If I were you, I'd quietly let them."

The Roman elite were clearly not as interested in the entertainment value of my story as Agrippa II had been, and after putting it off for two years, someone finally admitted it was never going to happen. Whether they went through any official procedure to dismiss my case, I'll never know. As far as I was concerned, my confinement simply dissolved.

My guard went on, "We're paid up on rent through the end of the month. You're all set until then." The guard had a sadness about him. He'd been with me for about two years. He'd heard me talk to countless people about Christ. He'd even let me talk to him directly about salvation a few times. He never scoffed at a word I said and seemed to genuinely want to believe in Jesus. But he was never ready to give up the social structure he was so accustomed to, even for eternal salvation. He seemed to leave the house that day with a vague sense of having lost something.

It may sound odd, but my initial reaction to my new freedom was complete disappointment. I'd expected to go in front of the emperor and preach the gospel. I was fairly sure he would have wholly rejected Christ and ordered my execution. I mean, Nero, have patience to consider the Way? Stranger things have happened, but *Nero?* So I hadn't expected any direct traction with the emperor, but I had believed my case would spark sensation throughout the Roman Empire, maybe even bring respectability to Christianity. I had expected my death to be my crowning achievement for Christ. Stephen's death still influences me (if I hadn't played such a direct part in it, I would dare say "inspires" me), even this late in life. I know it sounds silly, but I was beginning to feel slighted of a great ending for my story.

I pulled myself back together with the practical "Now what?" question. Rome had been such a major focus for me for so long that I considered sticking around. Firmly, and I mean *firmly,* establishing the gospel here would propel it throughout the entire world. But I wasn't the one to bring the gospel to Rome. As an apostle who was commissioned directly by the voice of Jesus, I, of course, had authority in Rome as I do in all churches. Still, Rome wasn't my baby, and through the Holy Spirit, I had to consider what would be best for the Church as a whole.

I had come to Rome as commanded. I had wrapped up all the little loose ends that my letter to the Romans had not previously taken care of. There had always seemed to be a gulf between the Roman church and the other, better established churches following Jesus. By the time of my vague release from arrest, I had become the common thread, stringing the Roman church together with the others.

This isn't to diminish Peter's efforts for the Lord, and there's no telling how much his efforts indirectly aided mine. Plus, he has almost surely brought more Jews into the Way here than I have. But before Peter and his follower Linus became Rome's leading figures, my efforts had synced the church in Rome with the rest of the Church; I'd first straightened it out theologically so that it was on common ground with the other churches. (Of course, Peter's work must have also helped with this.) I had established elders in the Roman church who were true followers of Jesus, not simply self-important preachers. I had then made a conscious effort to introduce the Roman Christians and especially these leaders to Christians of outside churches so they could grow together instead of apart.

It isn't going too far to say that my efforts in Rome provided the keys to the Church's functioning as a single organism. While Peter focused on bringing individuals in Rome to Christ, I picked up where James had left off, connecting the churches as I'd seen him connect Antioch to Jerusalem. Rome wasn't my baby, as I can claim about many other churches. (In fact, at this point, it looks pretty clearly to be Peter's.) It was a vagrant toddler that I persuaded into a functioning part of the larger Christian society.

I could clearly see the good I had done in Rome. But I had done so much more in so many other places.

I'd envisioned an audience before the emperor to be much like my experience before Agrippa. But Agrippa was responsible for the Jewish world. The emperor was responsible for the whole world. The world looked much bigger from Rome, which meant I was that much smaller. To put it in perspective, during my imprisonment, while I fantasized about appearing before the emperor, the Celtic queen Boadicea led Britannia in a fiery revolt against Rome and burned much of Londinium. Next to such empire issues, how could little Paul, who was unfairly treated by the Jews, expect any real attention?

So, standing there alone in the house after my jailor left, absurdly dejected for having not been executed, I pondered my next move. My fizzled-out Roman visit had left me out of gas. When I really considered my situation from all angles, there didn't seem any use to remaining in Rome at all. I was too little to gain access to the high and mighty of the great city to preach the gospel to them and too big to sit by the established churches in town while the properly appointed elders worked according to their functions.

I could go to Spain! I had thought of this before, and it appealed to me greatly—a fresh land where the gospel had yet to be preached: arguing with pagans, bringing people into the Way, establishing churches—I smiled—correcting their misjudgment, fighting the schismatic tendencies of the strong-willed, and getting all the different personalities to work together for a smoothly-run church. Corinth flashed in my mind. I became tired.

I had already founded many churches throughout the world and struggled through those raging fires, painstakingly quenching each one until not an ember remained. Looking back while thinking of Spain, I realized just how much work it had been, and I wasn't confident that I had enough in me to go forward for another round.

Yet, going back didn't seem like it would be particularly productive either. I had established leaders quite capable of quenching any little flare-ups that might occur now. They didn't need me. Ironically, this led me to the slightly huffy and inaccurate feeling that the leaders I'd established were turning me out. And after having been so tired by the idea of Spain, I now thought indignantly, "I've still got more to offer!"

Then, back to home base. I would go to Syrian Antioch and to Jerusalem, not really distinguishing which one I considered home base. But really, neither would look at all like it had when I had last seen it. The churches had grown, the apostles had moved on to develop other local churches (or had been killed), and the local elders had appointed new people to execute the churches' functions. The Lord's brother, James, was among those killed. He'd been thrown off one of the Temple's lower roofs and then finished off with clubs. Both Syrian Antioch and Jerusalem would be completely different.

I lingered between returning to the established churches, pushing forward to Spain, and remaining in Rome. I spent a couple of days in this indecisive haze, which really didn't suit me, when one of Timothy's younger friends from the north of the city came to visit.

He was elated to learn of my freedom. "You have to come to the north side! We have a house, and some people listen to us." His youth betrayed a warning that I could be moving into a flop house, but with his determination, it also suggested that an older, more-established personality could lend them the legitimacy they needed to really be effective.

Because the option of staying in Rome looked the easiest—I guess it's my nature—it became the least appealing. The idea of acting as a mentor in Rome felt like a tether. I began to get that creeping itch to move, thinking then of the West, now of the East. Settling in with these youths was not the thing of my daydreams. However, it slowly sank in that this new place could serve as a home base for missionary trips to Spain. Sold!

Spain

As I thought more on Spain, I grew more excited. It was wide open country for evangelism. It would be just like the good old days when every inch of ground won had been hard won. As I contemplated, I came to the conclusion that this was my one real strength: fighting.

Most of the other apostles seemed much better able to settle into a place of calm and preach than I could. When I thought back to the places I had "settled into," I realized I'd never really stayed anywhere long without a direct conflict to resolve. When I thought I'd found an exception, like Ephesus, I realized that I couldn't really say I was peacefully settled there because I had only used it as a base to launch myself into the controversy and fight of establishing churches in the surrounding area. What was wrong with me that I was the only one not at peace with being at peace?

Now, with Spain before me, I would be able to set aside this useless self-reflection and get back to what I was good at: fighting. I could land at Tarraco or even sail through the straits of Gibraltar to Gades. I even began to think that I could do Gades and the surrounding area first, and then after a quick refresher in Rome, go to Tarraco and its surrounding area. Over years of further visits, I could expand those "surrounding areas." Who knows? In ten or fifteen years, I may be able to cover all of Spain!

All of Spain! Pth!

I did take two trips to Spain during my year of freedom in Rome, first to Gades and then to Tarraco. My long-hoped-for Spanish mission proved an absolute bust. I tried to keep a stiff upper lip with the Gades disaster and told myself it wasn't so bad. With this attitude, I deluded myself into the trip to Tarraco, but after Tarraco, it became impossible to deceive myself.

I would not be converting all of Spain to Christ. I would not be an instrumental part in converting Spain. I would not be able to establish any church in Spain. Spain was not "just like when I started."

After Gades, I tried to joke with myself, "At least no one beat you up." But really, that had been the problem at both locations: nobody cared enough to beat me up. I couldn't get anyone to feel any emotion, one way or the other.

There wasn't any real Jewish presence in Gades or Tarraco, so no synagogue, at least that I could find out about, which meant no real starting point from which to gain steam. Lack of Jews also meant there was no one to find Christianity offensively blasphemous, so my message inspired no deep-seated, angry emotion to stir up attention. Trying to start in a plaza, I quickly learned that even the Spanish who could understand Greek simply weren't interested in big discussions like Greeks or Jews or even Romans. In the surrounding area, not a soul could understand a word any of us said. Either that or they simply pretended not to.

Letting myself go to Tarraco after the Gades fiasco was an absurdity built on unrealistic daydreams of reliving a romanticized past. It may have been my failure to listen for the Holy Spirit, but I was just so uncertain of which way He wanted me to turn. It is very embarrassing to write this, but there's no possible way to spin it. At least going to Spain broke up my time in Rome, not that it was long before I started getting antsy again. Plus, there is the possibility that God will use my efforts in Spain in a way that I just can't see. But that seems like a major stretch.

Ultimately, there I was, settled in Rome, feeling unsettled. I wanted to move and be productive but saw no use for myself anywhere.

Fire

The fire started in the night at the Circus Maximus between the Aventine and Palatine hills in south-central Rome. The Circus is (or maybe I should say was), of course, a giant stadium. And like all stadiums, as the bleachers ascend to ever higher levels, there is increasing space under them. Here in Rome, where real estate surrounding such an entertainment complex is so valuable, it would be ridiculous to leave all that space under the bleachers of the massive Circus unused. Shops were built in, surrounding the Circus under its bleachers facing out to the street.

Some of the shops under the bleachers targeted Circus goers, often paying a premium to be closer to the entrance, but all types of shops sold to the public. Several of these shops sold flammable liquids, which didn't help matters, especially because the whole wooden complex was basically built of kindling. Once the fire started and a little wind whipped up, an inferno was inevitable.

The fire grew stronger throughout the day and was still raging the following night when I went to bed. It remained safely to the south, and even if it gained some more momentum over the night, the Romans would too; they'd have it under control in the next few days, and the few districts that suffered the tragedy could start the rebuilding process per the norm.

When I awoke on the fire's second day, I casually wandered through the strong wind to the market for news. I wasn't the only one out for news; the market was quite busy with the agitated and excited. I didn't even have to ask what had happened; several people were so eager to yap about information they may have only just gotten that they bombarded me: "Did you hear? Did you hear about the fire?"

Fires, even major fires, are fairly common in Rome. But this one spread faster, wider, and in more directions than any other, at least in our generation. The fire gained a firm hold on at least four districts in southern Rome and practically wiped out the district of the Circus. It reached the Tiber River and wrapped around the Aventine Hill early the day before and even blew up the city's southernmost hill to some extent by evening.

The fire completely evaded all Roman efforts of hindrance. Every time they tried to concentrate their efforts to gain ground, the wind twisted, and the fire marched in a different direction. In that first thirty-six hours or so, the fire became bigger than any the Romans had ever dealt with.

I listened quietly as my reporter went on and on with an excited flourish of gestures. There was the report of panicked people causing more confusion and making matters worse. There was the possible but seemingly too poetic report of people giving themselves to the fire out of grief because it had already consumed all their worldly goods. There was the report about the looting. I wasn't all that interested in this gossipy level of detail, but this chatterbox was on a roll, so I didn't interrupt him.

"And there was this group, like a gang, that wouldn't let people put out the fire or protect their stuff! They defended the fire with violence and even threw torches to help accelerate it!"

This was odd. Open arson? With the threat of the death penalty? And continuing even after the blaze was in full force?

"They were looters. They must have been. That's the only reason I can think of for doing it," he theorized.

But then, when the fire was in full blaze, why were they not concentrating on looting?

"And they kept shouting, 'I have authority!' and, 'One has given us authority!'" My heart froze. "Like, who's going to give authority to burn up the city? Nero? The senate? Can you picture the senate sitting around, talking about the benefits to Rome of burning the city down?" He became so distracted with this concept, which he found comical, that he began to impersonate the pompous senators. To thank him for the information, I forced myself to smile at his inappropriate flippancy; then I excused myself.

Who would have given authority for arson? It could have been looters or general rabble, troublemakers inventing an excuse to not be arrested or killed for their actions. But if looting was their purpose, why not focus on looting where the looting was good? And if they were just troublemakers looking to escape punishment, why not just slip off into the chaos and disappear once the blaze roared?

My informant was right; it was ridiculous to think the senate was behind the blaze. Even if they had some nefarious purpose that they could justify to themselves, they would have had to discuss it openly enough to bring political destruction on their heads. But what about Nero? He could have given the command without anyone but the commandees knowing it. All gossip aside, Nero really is just a spoiled brat with no concept of value or costs. True, he likes gold and goodies, but it's all easy-come-easy-go to him. That's how he treats his wealth, and that's how he treats his people. I'm sure he wouldn't hesitate to start a fire if he thought it would benefit him.

There is a rumor, now prevalent, that Nero caused the fire as an excuse to rebuild on a grand scale. The rumors go so far as to say that he wanted to rename the city Neropolis. He has, in fact, started construction of a palace absurdly over the top in grandeur, lending credibility to the rumor. On the other hand, I suppose he would have rebuilt so wastefully even if the fire was just a convenient chance. Either way, he couldn't give a hoot for anyone else's life or property, so it wouldn't even be that shocking to learn he gave the order simply because he was bored and wanted to see some action.

Still, it didn't seem to add up. If Nero had given the order, wouldn't those who had been ordered to burn also have been ordered to keep their mouths shut about where the order came from? And again, when confronted after the blaze licked the sky, why didn't they just slip off into the chaos without a word of explanation? If they had been pinned down and forced to explain for their lives, why didn't they say, "Nero gave me the command" instead of the vague "I was given authority"?

I turned it all over, again and again, and even thought up wild scenarios wherein the "authority" could have come from an outside king and things like that. But when it came right down to it, if the reports were right, there seemed to be only one logical and clear answer that fit just perfectly.

Christian Rome had begun before Peter, I, or any of the other apostles had been in the city. Strife between these Christians and the non-Christian Jews created a sense of unity among the Christians for a while, but the sense of unity allowed false gospels and bogus teachings to abound. One group of self-proclaimed Christians coagulated around the belief that Christianity suited their political motives. To them, "freedom in Christ" equated to "Down with Rome!" and we were back to the military messiah.

I had known of the prevalence of this anti-Roman sentiment as a false teaching about the Messiah in the Roman church before I ever set foot in Rome and had even written a letter to the Roman Christians to stamp it out. The letter was written to deal with a host of issues coming out of the Roman Christian community, and at the time, this anti-Roman rebellious streak didn't stand out from all the other issues the Roman church was going through. It seemed like a completely unkindled, harmless spark to ears that had spent so much time in rebellious Jerusalem. I did address the issue in my letter, though briefly and only at the end. I explained that those who have earthly authority have it from God, so, in general, it is rebelling against God to rebel against the earthly authority.

When I first heard of the arsonists claiming "authority," shock and embarrassment lashed me. I even suffered a momentary sense of guilt. I'd been in Rome for over three years and had not dealt with this pseudo-Christian political belief. Then again, I hadn't dealt with it because it had never come up, so I had no way of knowing it was still an issue. Had this belief lingered out of sight? Had a small, rebellious group of Christians splintered from the local church to cling to their militant stance after my letter? Could I have missed something so glaring? The arsonists may have been a group with one of these heretical opinions that managed to stay together even after they left our community.

I tried to find more information about this group of anti-Roman Christians, but it was useless. They never played a significant part in the local church. My friends, whom I now quizzed on the topic, described them as a handful of young guys. They spoke in the church a couple of times about the freedom of Christ and how being subject to Christ meant the emperor could never hold any power over them. They didn't attend meetings regularly, but whenever they were in a conversation with Christians, the topic was always Roman oppression or the frivolous waste of Nero or the senators. They were angry young men who had little interest in the peace of Christ. Because their attendance was so irregular, no one really noticed when they stopped coming, but most of the people I talked to guessed it was sometime shortly after my letter was read.

Based on all the information I had collected, I felt pretty sure I knew who had caused this fire. They weren't necessarily Jewish, but it's as clear as the bright star of David that they were familiar with the Jewish concept of the savior, the Christ-to-come, the military messiah. Bumps in taxes over the past couple of decades had made sure that this view remained alive and well, if not dominant. They hoped for and expected a military savior to arise and destroy the Romans or at least to free the Jewish people from the Roman fist. When they learned of the Lord and Savior Jesus Christ, they came running to Christianity. When they learned that the Church didn't hold their political views, they wrote Jesus off as a hippie, too chicken to fight, and had nothing more to do with the Church.

What is less clear, but somewhat probable, is that these angry young men still clung to their belief in a supernaturally aided overthrow of the Romans. After leaving the local church, these men had no further connection with Christianity, as they had no interest in the hippie Jesus. Their mysticism must have grown so extreme that they thought they were aiding a military messiah, that burning Rome was their duty under this supernatural authority.

These arsonists may have even called themselves Christians. Christianity and Judaism are now seen as separate even by the Romans, but it isn't like the Romans to bother about the details of our religious differences. It's hard to guess if the Romans will blame the Jews who expect a messiah or the Christians who claim to have a messiah. They won't bother distinguishing between the followers of Jesus and groups of violent messiah mystics; Rome will simply blame all the Christians or all the Jews. Or both.

Later, as I discussed this with a small group of friends, one of the youngest pointed out, somewhat cynically, "Any Roman with a vague understanding of a messiah freeing the Jews could certainly have used it as a setup if he wanted to clear land for a palace or if he just plain hated the Jews. Or hated the Christians."

I had to admit that he was right, which put us back to square one: it could have been anyone who started that fire. Unfortunately, as reports of the gangs who had been "given authority" increased in circulation, so did the likelihood that this fire was going to be blamed on either the Christians, the Jews, or both.

The fire burned for two days and two nights, and the Romans seemed no closer to stopping it or even slowing its progress. The home where I had been under house arrest was almost certainly destroyed now, along with most, or even all, of the homes in that area.

The rebuilding effort that was sure to come might be a good place to meet people to bring to Christ, but would it be too many people? I would have loved to help with the rebuilding effort, but every pair of hands came with a mouth. The destruction was vast enough at this point that getting food to those mouths might be problematic... and I had nothing to help that. Also, by the time we started rebuilding, would I have a place to live, or would it, too, have been consumed?

Then, something else struck me that night as I lay in bed. With so many residences destroyed, rent would go sky high. Whether I could scrape up the cash was beside the point. Rome wasn't a cheap place. Where I was staying was considered "low rent," but by Roman standards, that didn't mean much, and now rent would surely soar.

I decided to get all the information I could in the morning and then consider my options. Having made indecision my decision, I relaxed enough to fall asleep. But it proved an uneasy sleep.

The morning of the fire's third day brought more of the same information: more fire and more destruction. The only real news was that the Romans had begun to talk about destroying some houses before the fire got to them. The plan was to make a line, many properties wide and many more long, of desolate ground that the fire would be unable to pass. Many prominent Romans lived beyond this line, and thus, their properties would be saved. Selfishly driven as it was, there may have been no other option to save even a part of the city this side of the Tiber River.

That was it, then; I was going to leave the city and head west. With the decision made, I was eager to get on the road ahead of as much traffic as possible. I packed up my sparse belongings, made hasty goodbyes, and crossed the northernmost bridge over the Tiber River with Titus, among several other believers, making it out of the city several hours before noonday.

From the Fire

The countryside west of Rome was littered with people, and I imagined it must have been swarmed to the south. I spent the late morning and afternoon walking to Rome's nearest port city, Ostia. I hoped to take a ship from there to just about anywhere in the right direction, by which I mean anywhere but Spain.

When I made it to Ostia, I was surprised to find it so busy. I mean, I expected busy, but the city seemed to burst at the seams with people. The market was packed with displaced Romans; many had taken up lodging in the town, and many more were inquiring about it. The town was so packed and everything so busy that I began to get nervous about finding a ship to carry us from the chaotic Ostia.

As it turned out, Titus didn't have much trouble securing us passage on a ship that was all loaded up and ready to go. The ship wasn't leaving until the next morning, but when Titus returned to the market and saved me from another "what-they-should-do" conversation about the fire, we departed and went aboard the ship. In the morning, we would sail for Crete, which is probably why Titus was able to secure passage. Nobody wanted to go to Crete, but we wouldn't have to stay long and could go anywhere from there. Plus, we had a safe place to sleep for the night.

Crete

Our ship stopped in Crete to exchange cargo, and the captain informed us that he planned to leave for Tarraco, Spain, the next day, soliciting us to buy passage. No thanks! It looked like we would have some time on the island waiting for another ship.

I have to admit that I scoffed and grumped at being stuck on the island of the notorious Cretans (but not quite as much as I scoffed at returning to Tarraco). These people counted the quality of a person according to the cleverness of his lying and cheating. But Titus beamed with glee. "There's nowhere to go but up!" he said. And why not? It had never crossed my mind to stop and evangelize at Crete, even though I'd sailed past the island many times and had even been there as a prisoner on my way to Rome.

Encouraged by Titus's optimism and energized by his relative youth, I went with him into the city Gortyn. The walk into town was a bit of an eye-opener for me. It seemed that Titus was leading, and even more oddly, I felt content to follow. I wasn't having trouble keeping up or anything like that, quite the opposite. It was as if he had taken a heavy pack off my shoulders so that I could keep up with his swift pace.

Titus and I preached the gospel in the market for two days and found the number of Cretans interested in the Word shocking. At the end of that second day, we were invited to Knossos's home for the evening and were begged to explain more on the third day. I hesitated to follow this Cretan who claimed to be a new believer home because, well, I just seemed to hesitate more. But Titus snatched up the opportunity without even a glance of consultation in my direction. Of course, he was right; the door was open, so we had to go through. We couldn't leave them hanging and open to perverters of the Truth, as they were at this point. I felt a little tired, but I knew we had to work to establish these people.

The next day at Knossos's house proved exciting. In my younger days, I might even have been amused by the situation that unfolded. The group gathered over the course of a couple of hours, and during this time, we were hammered with questions. The questions all seemed pointed, and the audience was intently interested in listening to what we had to say.

Then, a Cretan named Ulysses began to speak in a low, sincere tone. Shifting his weight from leg to leg, he explained that he was the head of the Unknowing Believers, a group with a strange bond.

"Our parents came to each of us, telling us that the gods were wicked," he said. "They told us that there was only one God and that this one God was the world's Savior. This was all they could tell at the time, but they demanded we keep silent because of the sacredness of this mystery. In consolation, they promised to fill us with the knowledge of Jesus, who would give us the path to eternal life in a very short time if only we held our tongues for the moment. We complied, but the next day, Roman soldiers invaded each of our houses and dragged our parents off for claiming that Jesus, not Nero, was Lord. They confiscated all our property, and we haven't a penny for a breadcrumb…"

"Shut up!" yelled our host, and before we could be shocked at his verbal response, Knossos punched Ulysses in the eye. Ulysses stumbled backward and fell to the floor. "Get out, you *****!" our host yelled without discretion. Ulysses scrambled to the door with the other Unknowing Believers, but as he got to his feet, I swear he was grinning.

About a third of them left, and a few moments passed in silence. Then, our host made a loud announcement: "Anyone else who's here for money can get out too! They haven't got any, and even if they did, I wouldn't let you take it!" After a couple of awkward seconds, another third of the people left. Interest in our Lord was significantly less than it had appeared.

On one hand, our host had cleaned house so that our efforts wouldn't be wasted. On the other, he was verbally and physically violent in the process, not exactly the image we were going for as Christians. How in the world was I going to address this? But I didn't have to, for Titus began to speak before my head had cleared. He politely asked our host if he could relate a story about our Lord. Receiving permission, he went into the story of John the Baptist, which was completely unconnected to the events we had just gone through. Titus understood that a "turn the other cheek" conversation at this point would not be helpful and might even alienate those now ready to listen to the gospel.

As Titus spoke, a wave of self-doubt washed over me. As these events had unfolded, I'd simply stood dumb in my uncertainty. If I was so shaky with basic liars and punk squabblers, how useful could I still be?

I was beginning to feel my age a bit or at least beginning to realize that it was my age I had been feeling for some time now. But before I had a chance to dwell on it, Titus pulled me back into the conversation.

That night, my thoughts of inadequacy came back in full force. I want to be clear that my feelings at this time were in no way feelings of hopelessness but rather a somber sense that my part had been played. I felt as if I were being promoted to an easier position, which is the same thing as being demoted to a position of lesser responsibility. I thought and prayed very deeply that night about the changing of roles that was taking place by the will of the Lord and despite my resistance.

My work for the Lord wasn't done. In fact, in big-picture terms, not much had changed. I would still go where the Lord's work needed to be done. I would still be bold for Christ. I would still preach the Word. And I would still take a beating if necessary. But I was older now. I had watered and nurtured new church leaders that the Lord had planted. Their fruit was ripe, and those who would listen could feed on them.

This was exactly what I had planned and worked for, but it had happened so smoothly that I hadn't realized the transition was now more or less complete. The next generation of leaders was now fully competent and ready to step up.

So what was I? An adviser? A relic?

I decided I could go back and be a relic in the Promised Land as well as I could be one in Crete, so I put together a loose plan. I would take the first ship that could get me to Syrian Antioch or Jerusalem. I would visit both cities and then work my way through the churches I had established. Titus would stay in Crete and work to establish the church there.

Jerusalem

As it turned out, the first ship that fit my bill traveled to Caesarea, so Jerusalem would be my first visit. I don't know what I had been expecting. I suppose it was something like I'd walk into Jerusalem, take a deep breath, and feel the Holy Land in my soul as a mother welcoming me home. What I experienced was significantly less pleasant.

Jerusalem was essentially the Jewish capital of the world. This was where Roman antagonism cut the most pain, and this was arguably where the Jews felt the strongest itch to rebel. I discussed the situation with the local church leaders, and it was clear to us all that it was only a matter of time before the Romans would have a full-scale rebellion to suppress. Destruction was coming. The only question was what part the Christians would play in the catastrophe.

Agrippa II was in Jerusalem at this point, and as a representative of the Christian community, I tried to see him. I went to the gates of the Herodian Palace with a letter requesting admittance. I had dictated the letter earlier that day, and it explained that I sought an audience to discuss the safety of the local Christians in case of a Jewish rebellion.

The guard who took the letter returned quite quickly and curtly dismissed me. Agrippa flat-out denied that any general uprising could possibly happen. Aside from a handful of lunatics, the Jews were "completely devoted to Rome." Any talk to the contrary was borderline treason.

The "don't press the issue" was clear in the message, so I left without argument. This was probably what I should have expected. For all his indecision and general refusal to face conflict, two things about Agrippa were crystal clear: He loved the Jewish people and had their best interest in mind, and he was 100 percent loyal to the Romans. He wasn't going to face the fact that a real conflict would erupt between the two groups.

As I walked away, the superficial pain of rejection faded, and I realized that the visit had actually been a major success. If the rebellion happened, Agrippa would not group the Christians among the rebellious. It wasn't clear how helpful this would be during a Roman rampage, but Agrippa would know that the Christians weren't aiding the instigators. If able, he might even provide them with sanctuary.

I returned to the local church leaders to inform them of my success. They had eagerly anticipated my arrival but were less thrilled with the news than I was.

"How could you have expected better than this?" I asked them. "Even if he had acknowledged the problem and promised to keep the Christians safe, in a situation of total rebellion he wouldn't do anything differently for us that he won't do now without such promises." The Christians in Jerusalem were in as good of a situation as anyone could hope for.

Unfortunately, even the best possible situation for a Jerusalem resident was terrible. I did get some pushback from the local church leaders who had evidently hoped way too much of my one visit to Agrippa. "Easy for you to say! You don't have to live here!" was their almost unanimous response, though most stated it more tactfully.

Of course, we all knew the real answer to the problem, and now was my chance to say it. "You don't have to live here, either." I was as clear and direct as possible without being confrontational. It was the only answer. Get out while the getting's good.

At this, everyone in the room sat back, blank faced. Apparently, they'd never even considered it. Then, Matthias smiled broadly and spoke up.

"Paul? Is that really you? The Paul who stood for Christ in the face of death and beatings? The Paul who stuck with *Corinth* for three years? How can you tell us to surrender Jerusalem? *Jerusalem*, of all places!"

The question was fair, and Matthias had delivered it with such exaggerated shock that its being asked served to lighten the mood, which everyone appreciated. I explained that we weren't turning our backs on the local church but saving it. If we were turning our backs on anyone, it was on those whom we could have turned to Christ.

"I'm just saying that getting out of Jerusalem and separating ourselves from the Jewish-Roman conflict is the best option. Obviously, no one has to go; it isn't a moral decision, but if you do stay, you must prepare for the worst. There is no safe political path to spare you from the coming chaos."

The room was still with silence. "That's it, then? Stay for the trouble or move out? If the choice is that clear, there isn't any sense in discussing it further," said Matthias, sounding more perturbed with the situation than with me.

I added, "Remember, though, Agrippa knows we are submissive to Roman rule. Where he is in control, Christians will have at least one figure in authority who understands our innocence. If he is forced from town, the safest course for you is to follow him. You might want to consider where he would go in such a situation."

Looking back, my statement was too academic because any Christian with family in other towns would simply go there. When I realized I wasn't adding anything of value anymore, I awkwardly cut myself off with a solemn nod as if my clumsy final statement had been something wise.

The issue was settled. I had done my part, and now it was up to them. The Lord had granted me a tremendous degree of peace in my role as adviser, and I thanked Him profusely for that in prayer. I felt needed and useful.

My feeling of peace only lasted as long as that feeling of usefulness. I had been eager to be in Jerusalem, and now I was eager to be in Antioch. I felt a twinge of sadness when no one seemed affected by my somewhat overly grand statement of departure; no one mourned my leaving or even suggested that they would miss me. I beat the sadness down before it flared into a pride issue. After all, this was a healthy thing. I hadn't planted the church in Jerusalem or painstakingly helped it to grow and develop. And most of all, I simply wasn't necessary there. Why should people make a big scene at my departure if they hardly knew me? This was a good, healthy church under competent leadership. They had recognized my authority so I could do my small part.

Now, it was time to move on. I had to somewhat force my expression of joy, however. I knew all that "it's good and healthy" stuff to be true, but it was hard to convert that knowledge into real joy.

Antioch, through the Churches, and Back to Rome

In Antioch, like everywhere else, tensions between the Romans and Jews were higher than normal. That said, the atmosphere of Antioch didn't come close to the fevered buzz of Jerusalem. Everything felt rather calm and routine; no critical issue existed to pull me in as a useful contributor. The people treated me respectfully and even seemed grateful for my previous efforts for the Church, but no one turned to me for help now. I wasn't needed.

The lack of a significant problem to handle set that all-too-familiar sense of agitated restlessness upon me. All in all, my visit was as pleasant as could be without controversy, but how could I crave controversy? It must be sinful to want problems. Was my inability to relax a sin that I'd been carrying for years?

No, of course not. It didn't take long to think and pray through this. I did not want controversy to exist. Although I had worked to bring controversy to the surface so that it could be addressed, I'd never created it. I just wanted to be useful, and fighting controversy had always been where I was the most useful.

The world had changed. My part was done. I was now useless. Everyone else seemed to know I was useless before I knew it myself, the realization of which embarrassed me greatly. For how long had I been bobbling around pretending to be effective for the Lord while everyone else could see how silly I looked?

Of course, this perspective distorted the truth in a petty way, but it was the starting point for my last real period of personal growth. I wanted to yell, "I still have more to offer!" But I'd been out of the picture in Antioch for over seven years by this point, and really, what a blessing that others also have so much to offer.

I spent a morning alone, walking through Antioch in somewhat of a sulk. Slowly, a sense of peace found its way into me. I'd started the morning feeling written off as burnt out. Over the course of my walk, though, my sense of being a smoldering, burned-out heap was replaced by the Holy Spirit with a sense of completion, a sense that my fire, a torch, had been passed. It was time to catch my breath and relax, not to be jealous for the flame.

This sense of peaceful completion has followed me for the rest of my life. From Antioch, according to the plan, I traveled back through the churches I had established. I could plainly see I was no longer needed in these churches, which now provided me with a sense of peaceful joy; the prick in my side felt soothed. On top of that, the greeting I received in these churches was one that a father, or maybe even a grandfather, would expect. The reunion atmosphere compounded my joy, leaving me almost jolly.

I accidently left my coat, some books, and papers in Troas, and there was a small flare-up with a coppersmith, but that's the worst I endured on my travels until a couple of months after I arrived here in Ephesus. Today, although that peaceful joy in my soul cannot be disturbed, any lasting joviality has vacated my being with the news that a general persecution of Christians has begun in Rome.

Evidently, the Roman fire of several months ago did not go well for Nero politically. True or not, the rumor that he had ordered the fire began to gain popularity, so, in turn, he is going all out, blaming Christians for the blaze. News of the worst atrocities being committed against Christians, even wild things, are coming out of Rome. Yes, arsonists are normally burned to death for their crime. But Nero is having Christians nailed to posts, covered in pitch, and burned for light to display his chariot skills as he rides about in the night. It's hard to distinguish the sober facts from outrageous exaggerations, but I know for sure the Holy Spirit calls me back to Rome to support my fellow Christians.

I am going to what might be the greatest challenge I've ever faced. I'm not excited for the fight, but I am excited to perform my duty for the Lord. Once again, I know I'm being led by the Holy Spirit.

Author's Postscript Regarding Paul's Death

Based on extra-biblical stories and tradition, Paul was arrested under Rome's general persecution of Christians during Nero's reign. At his hearing, Paul once again reminded the court of his Roman citizenship. This tactic didn't save his life, but it got him a second hearing because of a technicality where the court hadn't been prepared to properly try a Roman citizen.

After his proper trial, Paul's Roman citizenship also got him a somewhat more dignified death than other Christians; his head was cut off cleanly. Being killed at the same time as Peter highlighted the value of such an instant death. The Romans never miss a scrap of entertainment value at an execution, so realizing that both Peter and Paul, two major Christian leaders, were in their custody, they decided to make an event out of it.

Peter was crucified. Some reports say that he asked to be crucified upside down because he did not deserve the honor of dying the same way as the Lord Jesus and that this amused the Romans enough to grant him the request. This is questionable, as most reports do not mention Peter's being upside down. Either way, as Peter hung on the cross, Paul's head was cut off. For an encore to Paul's quick death, Peter's wife was brought out and killed. It wasn't a good time for believers.

Throughout his Christian life, Paul had always tried to emulate the qualities he had seen so perfectly displayed by Stephen. Although most of the qualities he admired in Stephen came naturally to Paul, one above all others particularly suited both men to the part the Lord had assigned them: the quality of waxing bold in the face of rising opposition. I have no doubt Paul went to his death filled with peace and joy, feeling honored for the opportunity to die, like Stephen, for his faith.

APPENDIX:

Historical Context

This appendix includes a fuller history than could be included in the narrative because, although that history is so crucial to understanding Paul's time, it would have bogged down the narrative too much to force it directly into our story. How the Jewish people thought, Roman-Jewish relations, the concept of the Messiah, the Jewish kingship, the office of the high priest—to name a few things—all have deep historical roots that I tried to address in the narrative. This appendix is for the reader who wants to go deeper without drowning in detail.

Israeli National History: Moses to the Return from Exile

Moses wrote the Torah—the five books of Moses, including Genesis, Exodus, Leviticus, Numbers, and Deuteronomy—for the Jews as God gave it to him. Modern scholars debate Moses's authorship, with most non-Christian scholars rejecting the idea. The most common belief is that the five books of Moses represent a mosaic of different authors from different time periods. Moses's authorship, however, was undisputed for over two thousand years; everyone in Paul's time accepted Moses's authorship and that, ultimately, the books had come from God. Everything right down to and through Moses was recorded in the Torah.

After Moses died, Joshua and Caleb led the Israelites into the Promised Land, conquered established populations, and settled the people in their new home. This was recorded in the book of Joshua.

At this point, there was no Jewish king; the twelve tribes of Israel all traced their lineage back to Abraham, but they operated more like a confederacy of twelve independent tribes. This was recorded in the book of Judges.

Then the people wanted to have a king because, you know, all the other nations were doing it. So, still before 1000 BC, in the name of God, the prophet Samuel anointed Saul, the first king of Israel.

A few decades later, God overthrew Saul and replaced him with David, the second king of Israel. God promised David that his dynasty would rule forever, but the meaning of this promise could not have been fully understood at the time. Both of Jesus's earthly parents descended from David, of course, so it is through Jesus that David's dynasty rules forever.

This was recorded, minus the Jesus bit, in the book of Samuel.

David had a long and prosperous time on the throne, as did his son Solomon, the third king of Israel. But when Solomon died, and David's grandson came to the throne, there was trouble. Rehoboam, only the fourth king of Israel, discarded the advice of the elders who had guided his father and took the hotheaded, tough-guy route that his young friends recommended.

Solomon had placed quite a burden on the Israelites to support his building projects, not to mention his lifestyle. (To his credit, Solomon built the first Temple for the Lord.) When he died, the people petitioned his son and successor, Rehoboam, for some relief. "Rehoboam! Please, give us a break! Cut back some of the work your father, Solomon, has placed on us." After considering the matter while enjoying the power of being king, he boldly announced: "My father may have put a heavy yoke on your neck, but I'll make it heavier! He whipped you with whips, but I'll whip you with scorpions!"

To this less-than-endearing statement, the bulk of the people replied, "Forget it!" and rejected Rehoboam as king. After all, they reasoned, Rehoboam was from the tribe of Judah, and they were from different tribes. Why should they let him continue as their king? Rehoboam maintained control of the southern part of the kingdom (the tribes of Judah and Benjamin) but the northerners (the other ten tribes) installed a new king over the rest of Israel.

At this point, God's promise to David that his dynasty would rule forever looked a bit shaky. (It is somewhat ironic that at the time of the split, David's line only controlled the Southern Kingdom of Judah and not the Northern Kingdom, which is referred to as Israel.)

This situation in which God's chosen people were split into two independent kingdoms existed for just over two hundred years when even greater destruction came upon them. The Assyrians defeated and captured the Northern Kingdom of Israel, including Samaria, which had basically become the capital city of Israel, in 722 BC. Great numbers of Israelites were killed, but great numbers were also forcibly taken from the Promised Land. The Assyrians deposited these Israelites across the Assyrian Empire, making it more difficult for them to amass a rebellion.

The Kingdom of Judea, the Southern Kingdom still ruled by David's descendants, lasted about another 140 years. Then, it was their turn. Nebuchadnezzar, King of Babylon, destroyed Jerusalem, tore down its walls, plundered and burned the Temple, and executed the king of Judea's sons before his eyes. After forcing the king to watch his sons' executions, they gouged out the father's eyes, ensuring that this would be the last image of the outside world the king ever had. The Babylonians killed huge numbers of Israelites and carried off all but the poorest people, distributing them throughout the Babylonian Empire.

(This is quite an abbreviated version that compacts the events of a drawn-out conflict. The reason this didn't kill off King David's line was because ten years earlier, Nebuchadnezzar had taken King Jehoiachin prisoner to Babylon and installed Zedekiah, Jehoiachin's brother, as his vassal king. Zedekiah then rebelled against Nebuchadnezzar. Eventually, about a decade later, this rebellion ended with King Jehoiachin's brother Zedekiah suffering the horrific sight and then losing his eyes but leaving King Jehoiachin able to continue the line of David.)

The two conquerors had decimated the Promised Land, plundering it for captives. They had thoroughly raked it over, spreading a thinned Israelite population over a much larger geographical area. In later times, still long before Paul was born, the Israelites of these dispersed communities came to be called the Diaspora.

The era of the kings, right down to the fall of Israel and Judea, was recorded in the book of Kings.

About seventy years after the Babylonians had dragged off the inhabitants of Judah to Babylon, Persia became the dominant power in the land. Cyrus, the great Persian leader, put an end to the Babylonian Empire when he sacked Babylon's capital city and laid claim to all the Babylonians called theirs. By this time, the Israelites had had plenty of time to settle into their new homes across what was now the Persian Empire, but the popular image of "back home in the Promised Land" and knowledge of family ties to the different tribes were far from extinguished.

When Cyrus and the Persians replaced the Babylonians as the Israelites' overlords, they allowed the Israelites to return to Jerusalem. Not all the Israelites returned to Jerusalem, and those who did, did so over a prolonged period. Several large groups returned under Israelite leaders Zerubbabel, Ezra, and Nehemiah and began rebuilding.

By about 445 BC, Jerusalem's protective walls had been rebuilt. The Temple had also been rebuilt and consecrated. Jerusalem came to be, more than any other city, considered the city of the

Jews, but many Jewish people remained spread throughout the Middle East, little islands within the various local cultures.

The return to Jerusalem was recorded in the books of Ezra and Nehemiah. Biblical books of Wisdom, Prophets, Proverbs, Psalms, and others were primarily written during the kingship and exile periods.

Return Home

When the Israelites were dragged off to foreign lands, they took the knowledge of their heritage with them. It was only seventy years after Judea was overcome that Persia prevailed and allowed the Israelites to return home, not long enough for biblical and family-history knowledge to have been lost.

Allowed to return, these Israelites didn't pour back in a massive flood to Judah. It was more like a trickle with clumps. The first clump brought all their exciting genealogies with them; there was no need to draw straws for positions. Zerubbabel, who led the return, traced his line back to King Jehoiachin of David's line. Jeshua, descendent of Aaron, returned with Zerubbabel, along with a host of priests and Temple administrators who were required to prove their family lineage before taking up their offices in the rebuilt Temple. Thus, they reestablished Temple worship with its positions filled by scripturally proper persons.

The kingship, on the other hand, carried a slightly different nuance. Upon returning to Jerusalem, it was one thing to claim the title "high priest" of some religion that the Persian king didn't really care about. It would have been quite another for Zerubbabel, whom the king of Persia had installed as his governor, to state bluntly that he was "king" of Israel. For the Israelite political leader to call himself king would probably have been regarded as an act of treason against the foreign king, sure to end in death.

By descent, Zerubbabel would have been king, but under the Persians (and later under the Ptolemaic Greeks and the Seleucid Greeks), the hereditary position of king wasn't relevant. The position of highest political power in Jerusalem at this time was that of governor for the foreign king. The foreign power filled this position with whomever they wished. It had no necessary tie to Israel's hereditary kingship, which faded out of relevant history until the birth of Jesus.

Hellenization: Takeover of the Greek World

In 336 BC, about one hundred years after the walls of Jerusalem had been rebuilt, the great King Philip II of Macedonia was assassinated. (Ancient Macedonia was basically modern northern Greece plus a bit of its bordering countries and stretching to the east.) Philip had won victory after victory in Greece. His military and political success was unprecedented in the West. But he was killed as he prepared to invade Persia, and his son, Alexander the Great, assumed the reins of power.

There couldn't have been a better replacement for Philip, the great conqueror. Alexander jumped into his new position and picked up right where his father left off. He overthrew the Persians and conquered the lands of Egypt, Syria, Judea, Galilee, and about everything else between Greece and India.

All the "greatness" of this military conquering was of much less interest to the first-century Jews than the Greekness that poured in behind the conqueror. It was not only Alexander's practice to found and settle new cities and populate them with Greeks but also to set up Greeks in existing conquered cities as he advanced.

Greek culture was very important to Alexander. After all, he had been educated by Aristotle, who had been educated by Plato, who had been educated by Socrates. Anyway, Alexander's conquering was nothing when compared to the Greek culture's conquering that followed in his wake.

At the height of his success, Alexander had a terrible, horrible, no good, very bad few days of fever and abdominal pain before he died. This left us with one of those obnoxious historical periods with millions of petty, little events that interfere with our succinct discussion, so we're going to cut to the chase. After Alexander died, most of the area he had conquered remained under Greek control, but the Greeks fought savagely and unscrupulously with each other. By about 300 BC, there were two empires important for Jewish history: the Seleucid Empire and the Ptolemaic Empire, each named after its founding ruler.

It's important to understand that although these empires were each thoroughly Greek in the sense that they concentrated all political power in the hands of Greek rulers, they were independent empires; they were separate from the political powers of Greece and Macedonia.

Once the dust had settled from Alexander's death, Alexander's general Ptolemy controlled Egypt, and Alexander's general

Seleucus controlled Syria, Lebanon, and farther east. The Ptolemaic and Seleucid Empires would pass down through hereditary lines. Greekness had swallowed up Egypt to the south and Syria to the north with the Promised Land smack dab between the two.

These two major world powers were in regular conflict for control of the Promised Land. As time went on, the Jewish people were under one Greek ruler now, the other later. For about 150 years, they were subject to these Greek rulers and the culture that had invaded all around them.

Greek culture had mixed with or overthrown just about everything in its way except the monotheistic religion of the Jews. Foreign gods aside, many elements of this new world would have been enticing. But after having been repeatedly rolled over, suffering all the ills of war, and considering the troublesome presence of those pesky foreign gods, the Jewish people largely rejected Greek influence.

As the Jews and the Promised Land were passed about, now under the Egyptian/Ptolemaic Greeks, now under the Syrian/Seleucid Greeks as it had been under Persia, no Jew dared call himself "king" without the express permission of the foreign ruler. The high priest's office, however, remained within the scripturally proper family. Temple worship continued.

All this changed when Antiochus IV, the Little Horn, prophesied in the book of Daniel chapter eight, ascended to the Seleucid throne.

Antiochus IV Epiphanes and the Maccabean Revolt

Antiochus IV, who called himself "Epiphanes" (basically meaning "the manifestation of a god"), made it a personal goal to free the Jews from their God. To help civilize them in Greek culture, Antiochus made Jewish practices illegal.

If the Torah or a circumcised child was found, the death penalty followed. Antiochus IV violently enforced the worship of Greek deities in all the Jewish cities. He even established idolatrous worship, sacrificing pigs in the Jewish Temple, which he had plundered (Josephus 1987, *A.J.* 12.5.4).

Although some of the Jewish people were attracted to certain aspects of Greek culture, Antiochus IV changed the game from the enticing "Isn't Greek culture wonderful?" to "You may not worship the God of your fathers." In so doing, he forced the Jews to pick sides—hold the line as God's chosen people or forsake God and melt away into the conquerors' culture.

The high priest Onias III's brother Jason offered Antiochus IV a great deal of money to be made high priest. Antiochus IV took the money, drove Onias III out of office, and installed Jason as the new high priest. And so began the foreign interference with the office of the high priest. (2 Maccabees 2004, 4.7-10)

Jason's money, however, couldn't buy Antiochus IV's lasting loyalty. When the pro-Greek Menelaus offered him a much greater sum of cash for the high priest position, which he would have to plunder the temple to pay, Antiochus IV simply replaced Jason with Menelaus. This removed the high priesthood a further step from the scripturally-appropriate person. (For good measure,

Menelaus had Onias III, the rightful high priest, murdered.) (2 Mac. 4.23-34)

Antiochus IV's reforms ignited a major revolt, started by a man named Matthias. He was overtaken by outrage when he saw a Jew preparing a sacrifice to a Greek deity. Matthias seized the Jew, slammed his body onto the altar, and killed him. Thus began the revolt that ultimately saved Jewishness. (1 Maccabees 2004, 2.23-24; *A.J.* 12.6.2)

Matthias died shortly after the revolt began, but the leadership of the revolt stayed within his family, known as the Hasmoneans or Maccabees. They continued to lead the Jewish fight for independence against perpetual outside threats.

During this revolt, the Maccabee family was able to reclaim the Temple for the Jewish people. The desecrated altar was replaced, and the Temple was cleansed. The Law required that the menorah in the Temple could only be lit with a special olive oil, and there was only enough to last one day, but the Jewish people needed eight days to get a new batch. The menorah was lit and—Praise God!—it miraculously stayed lit for the eight days required for obtaining more. (It is this miracle and the reclaiming of the Temple that Hanukkah celebrates. Though the eight-day-candle miracle is commonly known, it is neither in Josephus's account of events nor in either of the first two books of Maccabees.) (*A.J.* 12.7.6-7).

Over ten years after its kick-off, Jonathan Maccabees took over as leader of the revolt, and by then Syria had developed major internal problems. Antiochus IV had died, leaving his place claimed by two rivals, each needing as much help as he could get to secure rule. By this time, Jonathan led a formidable force, so the Syrian rivals competed to outbid each other for his help. In less than two decades, it was no longer Jews bribing a Syrian Greek for the high priesthood but Syrian Greeks bribing Jews for military support! One of the rivals won over Jonathan by, in part, installing him as the new high priest in Jerusalem in 153 BC. (*A.J.* 13.2)

Jonathan was succeeded by his brother Simon, and Simon's political rule over the Jewish people was accepted by popular decree, and also made hereditary (*A.J.* 13.6.4). Thus, at least by 141 BC, we can say that the Maccabee family, usurpers *par excellence*, had placed any kingship confusion behind them by fully taking over the role. And people certainly accepted this Maccabean dynasty. So the Maccabees became the kings of the Jewish people as well as their high priests. And like the high priesthood, the Hasmonean usurpation counters biblical propriety but claims some legitimacy by popular support.

The story of the Maccabean Revolt was recorded in the books of Maccabees (ironically, written in Greek). Two books of Maccabees make up part of the Catholic Church's Bible. Protestants and Jews reject their validity as Scripture, but the books are universally accepted as important works.

Establishment of Roman Dominance

Removing the high priesthood from its scriptural authority massively degraded it, and the kingship's Hasmonean shift also knocked it out of the proper hereditary line, but things got even worse when the Romans jumped in to stir the pot. It is true that the Romans generally left the Jews alone when it came to religious practices, but that wasn't enough for the Jewish people to accept Roman domination. The Romans excelled at drawing lines in the sand, and the Jews excelled at crossing them. The Romans held rule of the Promised Land, and the Jews resented any rule.

Pompey, the famous Roman general, secured Roman dominance by defeating Jerusalem with a three-month siege in 63 BC, after which he personally entered the most holy place of the Temple. From this battle, the Romans took a huge number of Jews to Rome. This significantly increased the size of the Roman Jewish community.

Pompey left the high priesthood with Hyrcanus II of the Maccabee family. But like the foreign rulers before him, he removed their right to use the title of king (*A.J.* 14.4.5).

From this point forward, Jewish and Roman politics intertwined tightly. Sometime after Julius Caesar defeated Pompey in civil war, he indirectly appointed a man named Herod to govern Galilee (*A.J.* 14.8.5 & *A.J.* 14.9.2).

When the dust of wars and conflict finally settled at the Battle of Actium in 31 BC, Augustus emerged as the soon-to-be Roman emperor. Herod, too, made it through the time of strife, and Augustus confirmed his position as king (*A.J.* 15.6.7).

Eventually, Rome delegated the power to appoint the high priest to Herod. By Paul's time, the king was not of the scripturally appropriate line of King David and was not popularly supported by the people. And the pro-foreign-overlord king chose the high priest from the pro-foreign-overlord social circle of Jews.

Herodians

Herod the Great baby killer, the first Roman-appointed king in the Promised Land, always feared losing power. (*A.J.* 14.14.4) In 30 BC, Herod killed Hyrcanus II, the elderly Maccabee and once high priest, once king, and the only person who could really challenge him for the throne (*A.J.* 15.6.2-3). Ironically, Herod had married a Maccabee as one of his many wives, and he often pointed to this marriage as enhancing his legitimacy. But he had her killed too (*A.J.* 15.7.4).

Toward the end of his life, Herod became so jealous of his throne that he had two of his sons killed for fear they would take it (*A.J.* 16.11.7). This was only a few years before the news of the Messiah's birth reached Herod, which set his fear and jealousy ablaze. The Jews universally understood that the Messiah would come as a military leader to overthrow the foreign rulers in the Promised Land, which would have put Herod out of a job, to say the least. His intelligence organization told him the Messiah had been born in Galilee, so he ordered the slaughter of all male children two years of age and under in that region (Matthew 2:16).

Very shortly after this attempt on the life of our Lord and Savior, Herod died from the most violent of punishments. He burned with an internal fever as he suffered a most insatiable hunger, and despite his eager food consumption, most of his body wasted away while his bowels and colon swelled in size and pain. His body tore open at the belly and rotted with worms while he yet lived (*A.J.* 17.6.5).

Before his death, however, Herod became deeply bitter that the event would be greeted with near-universal joy. He ordered the most prominent of Judea's young men taken to the Hippodrome. Then he ordered his sister, one of the world's few people who could rival her brother for wickedness, to have them all slain as soon as possible after his death. This way, the Jews would be forced against their will to grieve at his death (*A.J.* 17.6).

It is not clear if the soldiers guarding the young men simply refused to follow such orders or if Herod's sister failed to give them, knowing she would be held accountable. Whatever the case may be, the young men were released, which, of course, increased the joy at Herod's death (*A.J.* 17.8.2).

When Herod died during Jesus's infancy, the kingship got messy again. The title of king required the express approval of the emperor and the senate. After some chaos, including mass riot and rebellion that ended in the crucifixion of about two thousand Jews, the area that had been under Herod was split among three of Herod's sons. Half of it went to Archelaus, a quarter to Philip, and the last quarter to Antipas (*A.J.* 17.11.4). We follow Herod's line to Antipas because he holds prominence for Christian history, but was otherwise no more significant than his brothers.

Antipas received the title of tetrarch from the Romans, along with control of the lands of Galilee where Jesus Christ came from and Perea where John the Baptist's following grew. This Herod Antipas had married his half-brother's daughter and sister of the later-to-be-King Herod Agrippa I, named Herodias. (Evidently, there weren't enough Herods in the family without also making it a girl's name.) Herodias had divorced Herod Philip, Antipas's half-brother of a different mother, so the family tree was made up of knotty wood (*A.J.* 18.5.4). John the Baptist condemned this inappropriate marriage without reserve to his significant following, so Herod Antipas had him arrested and later ordered him beheaded (Matthew 14:1-12). It is also note-worthy, however, that Antipas would have seen a political threat in the rapid growth of John's following (*A.J.* 18.5.2).

Pilate sent Jesus to see Antipas, who was disappointed in his hope to see a miracle. Jesus refused to answer any of Antipas's questions and was sent back to Pilate. (Luke 23:6-12)

When Caligula became Roman emperor, he conferred the title of king unto the third generation of the Herodian line: Herod Antipas's nephew Herod Agrippa I. (This was after Caligula had released Agrippa from prison, Roman politics being what they were.) (*A.J.* 18.6.10). Over the course of his reign, almost all the land that had been under his grandfather, Herod the Great's, control came back together under Agrippa I (*A.J.* 19.5.1). This Herod Agrippa I was the one who had James, the brother of John, killed and Peter arrested in Jerusalem (Acts 12:1-5). Like his grandfather, he, too, learned the dual disposition of sniveling to the Romans and biting at all threats from those of lower station.

So the Jews in general did not find Herod's line endearing, and it was an outright plague to the Christians. This history made it easy to scoff at the kingship as either empty, ceremonial, or menial. This is especially true when you consider how loosely the position tied to the Jewish people at this time. In all fairness, though, there were several times when these political go-betweens, which may be considered part of the job beyond governor, provided significant service for the Jewish people.

For example, while the Romans expected the kings and administrators to keep the Jews under control, they didn't always make it easy for them. Emperor Caligula, who thought himself a living god, certainly would have ignited riots if his orders were followed to build a statue of himself in the Jewish temple. Agrippa I walked a careful balance to get Caligula to set the project aside (*A.J.* 18.8.7-8). The Herods' basely political personalities suited them perfectly for these tasks.

Herod Agrippa I's son Herod Agrippa II, before whom Paul appeared, possessed a much softer personality than his father's and great grandfather's. Agrippa II was only sixteen when his father died in AD 44 (*A.J.* 19.9.1). Emperor Claudius eventually gave him the title of king with a small area to rule too far north to matter much to most Jews (*A.J.* 20.5.2 & 20.7.1). At the same time, the Promised Land was again split up, and Roman procurators, or governors, were installed over it, including Judea. This is how Paul came to sit before Agrippa II, the king who, in spite of his title, hadn't any authority over the most important land of the Jews. Paul remained under the authority of the Roman Procurator-Governor Festus, who was charged with ruling over Judea, Samaria, and Perea.

(Paul's story in Acts breaks off in Rome around AD 62 or AD 64, and he may have been killed at that time. He probably died by AD 68 at the latest, while tensions were still building in Jerusalem.)

Agrippa II was still king when the angst and tension that had been brewing in Jerusalem and the rest of the Jewish world finally blew into wide-open rebellion as the First Jewish War. A few years into the war, in AD 70, the Romans destroyed the Jewish Temple (Josephus 1987, *B.J.* 6.4.1-8). The Temple's destruction represents the clearest severance point of the Jewish religion from Christianity.

The destruction of the Temple destroyed all the traditional worship that accompanied it, and the Jewish religion was forced to take a sharp turn to reestablish an identity. The world's eye had already begun to see the Christians as distinct from the Jews, and now the loss of the Temple felt like the destruction of everything Jewish. The outward appearance of Jewish practice fell away from the Jewish Christians, making them less distinguishable from other Christians. Some overlap lingered, and Christians later battled the heresy that the Jewish Scriptures didn't apply to them. That some living Christians came from a Jewish background fell quickly into irrelevance as a new segment of Christian history began.

Cited Sources

1 Maccabees. 2004. *The Apocrypha: The Apocryphal/ Deuterocanonical Books of the Old Testament.* New Revised Standard Version. Cambridge: Cambridge University Press.

2 Maccabees. 2004. *The Apocrypha: The Apocryphal/ Deuterocanonical Books of the Old Testament.* New Revised Standard Version. Cambridge: Cambridge University Press.

Josephus, Flavius. 1987. *The Works of Josephus: Antiquitates Judaicae.* Translated by William Whiston. Massachusetts: Hendrickson Publishers.

Josephus, Flavius. 1987. *The Works of Josephus: Bellum Judaicum.* Translated by William Whiston. Massachusetts: Hendrickson Publishers.

Afterword

I put this book together to be true to the Bible. The language throughout, including passages derived from the Bible, is my own as I judged most fitting for the tone of our story.

Over the past twenty-five years or so, my judgment on the life of Paul and biblical interpretation has been most influenced by the following, many of which I referred back to while writing this book.

(When it comes to the Old Testament Hebrew scriptures, I can't recommend the translations of Robert Alter highly enough. They are super easy to read AND professionally academic, a rare combination.)

"Acts: Keys to the Establishment and Expansion of the First-Century Church." *The Leadership Series 1*. Ames: BILD International.

Alter, Robert. 2016. *Ancient Israel: The Former Prophets: Joshua, Judges, Samuel, and Kings*. New York: W. W. Norton & Company.

Alter, Robert. 2004. *The Five Books of Moses*. New York: W. W. Norton & Company.

The Apocrypha: The Apocryphal/Deuterocanonical Books of the Old Testament. 2004. New Revised Standard Version. Cambridge: Cambridge University Press.

Archeological Study Bible. 2005. New International Version. Grand Rapids: Zondervan.

The ESV Study Bible. 2008. English Standard Version. Wheaton: Crossway.

Eusebius. 2022. *Eusebius' Ecclesiastical History*. Translated by C. F. Cruse. Massachusetts: Hendrickson Publishers.

The Jewish Annotated New Testament. 2011. New Revised Standard Version. New York: Oxford University Press.

Josephus, Flavius. 2022. *The Works of Josephus*. Translated by William Whiston. Massachusetts: Hendrickson Publishers.

The KJV Study Bible. King James Version. Nashville: B&H Publishing Group in 2012.

The New Oxford Annotated Bible with the Apocrypha, Expanded Edition. 1977. Revised Standard Version. New York: Oxford University Press.

"Pauline Epistles: Strategies for Establishing Churches." *The Leadership Series 1*. Ames: BILD International.

Philo of Alexandria. 2022. *The Works of Philo*. Translated by David M. Scholer. Massachusetts: Hendrickson Publishers.

Schaff, Philip. 2011. *History of the Christian Church*. Massachusetts: Hendrickson Publishers.

Schurer, Emil. 2012. *A History of the Jewish People in the Time of Jesus Christ*. Translated by Rev. John Macpherson. Massachusetts: Hendrickson Publishers.

Thank Yous

I'd like to thank Kathy VanDerkolk, MacKenzie Wells, and Jeanne Mansk for fighting their way through the original manuscript, which was, at best, a distractedly meandering story regularly interrupted by long, technical, historical passages. I can't tell you how helpful your heroic efforts have been in shaping this book.

Thank you to Jessica Andersen, my lead editor, who helped me develop an only slightly better manuscript into a much stronger and clearly focused book without sacrificing its individuality. Working with you was truly a pleasure.

Thank you to Jessie Cunniffe and Book Blurb Magic for focusing on every single word of my book summary and author bio—again and again and again until it was perfect.

Thank you to Nancie Struck for tying everything together with your professional insights in the final proof-read. I now know why your students fear your red pen.

Thank you to the Kinni Café and especially Angie, Brianna, Cara, Carol, Chelsea, Kay, Kim, Paula, and Sarah for supplying many eggs, toast, and coffee while I edited this book.

Likewise, I'd like to thank Cory and his team at Swinging Bridge Brewery for all the evenings that they brought a pint to my wife while she proofread this book.

Finally, to my wife, Jennica, for her help editing the book through its final stages. She has an amazing ability to point out my mistakes.

Fault for any errors that have made it through the editing process, of course, belong to Cory at the Swinging Bridge Brewery.

9 798868 500978